REDHEAD

Bedhead Book Two

KAYT MILLER

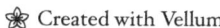 Created with Vellum

For the Beedle Babes.
You know who you are.

There are people you meet along the way that change your life. Make it better, richer. The women I met living on Beedle Drive remain some of the most important people in my life. Even though we're all busy with our families, jobs, and aspirations, I know that our bond will alway remain strong and constant.

I love you, ladies.

As for our Patsy , we lost her, sadly. Our Irish lass. The funniest person she knew. Cancer is a bitch —it took her from us way too soon. She was a force of nature and the life of the party.
We all love you, and miss you, Patty Jane.

PROLOGUE: LUKE

If you'd asked me a couple of months ago if I'd be in this predicament, I'd have laughed in your fucking face. Maybe I lacked the imagination needed to forecast the clusterfuck that is now my life, and that's on me. Hell, this whole deal is on me. The thing is, I'm not in any hurry to remedy the situation because I know if I do, she'll be gone. And by gone, I mean gone-gone. I don't want that. I want her here—just not like this. No, I need to figure out a way to nip this in the bud without upsetting the delicate balance that is Tayler and me.

God, I should be pissed as hell. What am I saying? I *am* pissed as hell, but she wouldn't understand because I've never really talked to her about my past. Since I met Tayler, we've talked a ton. Almost daily. And in that time, I've neglected to tell her why I am the way I am. Why I'll never be able to give her what she wants—love, a ring. I can give her sex, yes. I can fuck her all day every day, but that's not enough. It's all or nothing for her, and I get it. I hate the fuck out of it, but I get it. She deserves more.

So she's going about things in a new way. Tayler thinks she's being clever right now. She's wheedled herself into my world, the bar, all in hopes that I'll finally do something. That I'll commit.

But she's going about it all wrong. While she thinks changing the bar is going to make me happy, all it does is piss me off because it's the same as trying to change *me*, and that's never going to happen. My ex-wife figured that out the second I served her with divorce papers. I'm not changing. Not again. Not even for Tayler Sorenson. Nope, not even for her.

PROLOGUE: TAYLER

If you'd asked me a couple of months ago if I'd be in this relationship quagmire, I'd have scoffed in your face. Hell, three months ago, I was still licking my wounds after my ex-boyfriend, Dylan's, betrayal. I was in no way ready to take on something like Luke Green, but did that stop me from doing it? *Hell no.* And you want to know why? Ugh. I'm embarrassed to say it, let alone write it. I did it because Luke Green is *hot A. F.* For those of you who don't know what those last two letters stand for, they mean: *As. Fuck.* Luke Green is the poster boy for that little expression with his tousled, dirty-blond hair, rugged jawline, five-o'clock shadow, and tattoo-covered muscles. Oh, and let's not forget his broodiness. Luke's got the kind of bad-boy angst you only read about. With all of that in his proverbial arsenal, how could you blame me? I'm just an average girl. And average girls can't help themselves when there is a living, breathing Mr. Darcy-type guy leaning close to you, whispering in your ear all the dirty things he wants to do to you.

So, yeah. *Sue me.*

Honestly, if I could travel back in time, I'm not sure I would change anything. Well, sure, I'd change a few things, namely this shit with my ex that turned creepy. And maybe I'd even stay true to myself when it came to Luke.

Ha! That's a joke.

The man is my weakness. He's played me like a goddamn harp. I swear to you, I know less about Luke Green than I did that night we met back in September. How is that possible? I don't know. All I can say is the man gives nothing away. Not his past, not his memories, and certainly not his heart. And it's not like I haven't tried. I've tried just about everything to get the man to open up to me. I've been his friend, his lover, and right now, we spend almost every night together. Hell, I'm practically his roommate and still the man keeps his emotions in a proverbial vault.

Honestly, all of this "togetherness" is probably what's causing Luke's mood to take a dive. He's been extra salty lately—and that concerns me. A lot.

CHAPTER ONE

Luke: Three Months Ago

"Luke!"

I hear my name being yelled from the front of the house, the bar area. I know the voice. Quinn Maxwell, my newest hire, is calling for me. No doubt it's gotten busier since I've been holed up in my tiny office. She's got some dude in town from overseas who seems to be drawing a crowd. I'd better get out there.

"Yeah?" I say as I walk through the doorway wiping my hands on the bar towel that's always over my shoulder. The minute I spot Quinn, I give her a small smile.

"I want to introduce you to my best friend. A best friend I will never give free drinks to." Quinn pauses. "Promise."

Yeah, right. They always say shit like that, and they always give away beer to their "best friends." Ignoring my thoughts, I look left and spot her. My throat gets a little dry. Walking slowly up to the bar, I say, "Does your beautiful friend have a name?"

"Tayler," the gorgeous redhead says, holding her tiny hand out to me. "We've met, though."

My voice feels dry, scratchy. She's caught me a bit off guard, to be honest, because of course I recognize her. "I know. You were here last Wednesday."

"I... uh, yes, I was."

"You've also been here a number of times with a man." A short twerp who always had his eyes on other chicks. The fucking idiot.

Quinn responds quickly. "Her ex. He cheated on her. Can you believe that?"

"No." I stare at Tayler. She's probably the most beautiful girl I've ever seen with her pale complexion and those freckles. But even though she has sweet features, there's more to her than that. The woman is sexy as hell. "He's a fucking idiot."

"Right?" Quinn says, then laughs.

Ignoring her, I lean over the bar so I can get a little closer to Tayler just as she leans in closer to me.

This is getting good.

"Welp, I guess I'll move along." Quinn laughs again, then heads off to help another customer.

"So, Tayler," I say in my sexiest voice. "What're you doing later?"

"Ah, well...." She smiles, and it's so pure and real, it kind of takes my breath away for a second. "I've got a paper to write."

I give her my very best come-hither smirk. "Homework, really? You'd rather do homework than come home with me?" I'm not sure why I said that. I never take anyone home. I always go home with them; that way, I can do what I need to do and leave.

"I'm not that kind of girl," she says sweetly.

I'm about to laugh at her words because I've heard that line before, but this is the first time I believe it. "You're not, are you?"

She shakes her head slowly. "Nope."

Well, shit. Now what? "You're serious."

She nods. "I am."

This is surreal. First of all, I rarely proposition women. They do all the work up front. No, this is new. "Can I get your number?" I ask, and it surprises me. I don't take numbers. I don't give mine out either. Usually.

She tilts her pretty head to the side and blinks a few times. "Why?"

Why? She's asking why? "So I can call you."

"What would we talk about?" She's giving me her own smirk.

"Stuff." I mean, seriously? What I'd like to talk about is the many ways I want to fuck this girl, but I'm guessing that's not going to fly. "Maybe I can talk you into—"

"You won't." She sips her beer. "I just got out of a long-term thing, and I'm not going to jump into bed with the first guy who asks. It's not my style."

I'm the first guy to ask? Impossible. "What *is* your style?"

She sighs and starts to slide off her stool. I reach out and take one of her hands in mine. A tingle runs up from my hand to my shoulder and down to my chest. Swear to God, my nipples get hard. Embarrassing. "Don't go." I mean it. I don't want her to leave.

"That paper won't write itself." She chuckles.

Pulling her hand from mine, she holds her palm up. "Give me your phone."

Without a word, I grab it from my back pocket and set it in her hand. "Passcode is 1234."

She arches her pretty auburn brow at me. "Secure."

I shrug. I don't care about my security code. There's nothing on there that anyone would want. I don't pay bills with my phone or shit like that.

I watch as she types. Handing back my phone, she smiles again, and I want to wrap her up in my arms.

"If you want to talk, give me a call. Or text. But I meant what I said, Luke. I'm not into one-night stands."

"How 'bout two nights?" I chuckle. Worth a try, am I right?

She doesn't respond, just waves one little hand at me and turns to leave. I watch her hug Quinn goodbye and step out my front door.

Staring down at my phone, I bring up my contacts and laugh. She typed two words: Forever Girl. Now that, I *can* believe.

CHAPTER TWO

Tayler

The second I'm out the door of Cy's Roost, Luke Green's bar, I'm finally able to take a breath. No, I wasn't holding it, but it felt like it. I mean, the second he touched my hand, I thought I was going to pass out. It was that charged. How I kept my cool, I've no idea. A better question? How did I stop from going home with the man? Again, no idea. But I did. Hell, I even sounded sort of cool—aloof. Ha! What a joke. I'm the least aloof person on the planet. Control is the name of the game with me, even though inside I'm a frigging mess. I could blame my ex, Dylan, for some of that, but the truth is, I've needed to feel like I've had some kind of control over my life since I was fourteen.

I think it's what drove Dylan away, to be honest. I had him on a tight leash, as they say, most likely because he was my complete opposite and I thought I was doing what was best for him—for us. They say opposites attract, and I suppose that's the way it was with us. It was also our undoing. He wanted to go out, do fun stuff, while I wanted to stay in and make sure I kept my grades up. Sure, we went out now and then, usually to Cy's but sometimes to other bars too. His friends were douchebags and I never wanted to spend much time with them, so the last few months of our relationship, Dylan went out without me. That's when it happened. When he met *her. Savanna.* I should thank her. She helped end a four-year relationship that had gone stagnant.

I'm lying. I hate her. I hate *him.* No, that's not true. I love him in a fucked-up way. I'll probably always love him. He was my first, well, everything. First love, first sex, and first heartbreak. That last one sucks. Heartbreak is the perfect word to describe it because my heart literally cracked in half in my chest over Dylan.

To make matters worse, I had to do that all alone, without my best friend Quinn, since I angered Quinn so much so she wouldn't speak to me for weeks. Sure, I could have contacted her, but that wasn't our dynamic. For years she would always be the first to cave whenever we had a tiff. Not this time, though. This time she grew some balls somehow, and that meant I either had to crawl back and beg forgiveness or I had to deal with the end of my relationship with Dylan alone. Since I'm stubborn, I chose the latter. And it sucked.

Tonight, though, I feel... better. And not because hot Luke Green hit on me. It helped, sure, but it's all of it. I got myself out of my loungewear that I've been wearing for a few weeks, did my hair, and put some pretty clothes on so I could hang with my bestie and her new "friend." (We'll get to Cooke, the English rugby guy, in a bit.) I got gussied up to go out, and it made me feel like myself again. My life is a mess right now, but a night at Cy's is one step closer to normalcy.

As I left the bar, I hugged Quinn and told her to "make good choices." That saying cracks me up because honestly, I hope she makes a terrible choice tonight. She's held on to her V-card for far too long, and if she's going to lose it, she should lose it to a guy who flew halfway across the world to see her.

Sigh.

Dylan wouldn't have done that. Hell, he would barely drive to my parents' house while we dated. I always had to go to him, and we lived in the same town.

I wonder if Luke Green is that kind of guy. Would he travel a million miles to get to the woman he loves? Doubtful. From our interaction tonight, I think he prefers easy and convenient. Well, I'm neither of those things, sadly. For that split second, I almost gave in to my baser instincts with him, because I know sleeping with Luke would have been memorable. Probably life-altering. Hell, he'd probably put Dylan to shame (not hard to do) and also ruin it for my future husband or whatever.

Yeah, I bet sex with Luke Green would have been spectacular. But I'll never know.

God, I want to cry.

So I do.

CHAPTER THREE

Luke

"So, when's your friend stopping in?" I know I shouldn't ask my employee about her friend. Quinn isn't the kind of woman to let those simple words go. Hell, she'll probably call her and tell her I asked.

Is that such a bad thing, Luke?

"Which friend?" the smartass asks.

I throw the bar towel over my shoulder, lean my hip on the bar, cross my arms, and then glare at Quinn. "Tayler."

"Oh, Tayler? Hm, I'm not sure."

I know she's fucking with me because her voice just got all high-pitched and singsong-y. I sigh and move away from the bar. "Whatever." I attempt to act aloof, but she must know something. Her smile is more smirk than anything else.

"Just text her if you want her to come in."

"I...." She's pissing me off. "No need." Just trying to think of something to talk about since this place is dead. D-e-a-d. I swear, some Sundays are like this. It'll pick up later. There's a Packers game on the tube, so people will come in to watch that and eat some grub.

"She said you two have been texting a little bit."

So she *does* know.

"A little bit." But the redhead won't budge. I've asked her over to my place two other times, but she won't do it. I pick up two empty beer glasses from the bar and place them in the bin for dirty glasses. "She's stubborn."

Quinn snorts. "You have no idea."

I have some idea but I think I need a little backstory. Maybe Quinn will give me something I can use. "How long have you known her?"

"Forever. Elementary school."

"That's a long time." That long? She's got to have some good intel on my girl.

Not *my* girl. *A* girl.

"It is." Quinn nods, pouring a beer for one of the three customers we have right now. "We've been through a lot."

"She with that asshole for long?"

She turns her head to me, arching her brow. "You should really ask Tayler about that."

"You can't tell me how long she was with that cheating fuck?" I mean, seriously.

"Since junior year of high school. Four years."

Four years? That's a long time. I know because my marriage barely lasted two. "Wow." It's all I can think to say. Honestly, I can't figure out why Tayler wouldn't want to have an easy rebound. With me, of course. No one else. But you'd think it'd help clear her head. A reboot, as they say. Maybe that's my angle. Perhaps I should propose a rebound fling that can help her get over that douchebag and get on with her life.

I smile and Quinn sees it. "What?" she asks.

"Nothing."

"Luke, I've only worked here for a few months, but I can tell by your expression that you've got a plan."

I lose the smile. That's bullshit. Quinn Maxwell can't read my expressions. That pisses me off.

"And that one tells me you're mad." She looks away quickly. "Sorry," she mutters as she heads out into the bar to wipe down tables.

Yeah, run away. I don't want to be "figured out." By anyone.

ME: What are you doing tonight?

Forever Girl: Studying. Chem test tomorrow.

Me: Take a break. I'll feed you.

Forever Girl: Already ate but thanks.

I look at the clock. Three thirty. I just let Quinn go early because the place is dead.

Me: Dinner. I'll make you something for dinner.

Forever Girl: ...

I wait, staring at my phone like a puppy waiting on a treat. It's ridiculous. I need to man up.

Forever Girl: Ok. Sure. I could use a break. I'll be there around 6.

Hell yeah. She's coming.

What the fuck? When did I turn into a pussy over this girl?

Me: C U then.

Me: Bring your chem shit. I'll help you study.

Forever Girl: ...

She doesn't respond to that. Not a surprise. She knows jack shit about me. No one does, really. The fact that I was this close to going to med school out east is not something she knows about, and I plan to keep it that way. I can still wow her with my chemistry knowledge. Maybe that will be my in.

CHAPTER FOUR

Tayler

"You didn't bring your books?" Luke sounds almost disappointed about the fact that I came empty-handed. All I brought was my purse.

"You were serious?" I ask, looking a little incredulous.

"Yeah," he says with a pout. "I was a chem major."

I laugh because who the hell majors in chemistry? "You were a chemistry major?"

He leans back against the bar and crosses his arms. He looks a little perturbed. "Pre-med."

"You didn't finish?" I mean....

"Graduated with honors."

"From ISU?" I'm confused. Luke Green just doesn't seem the type.

He pulls away from the bar and steps closer to me. "I was headed to Johns Hopkins."

I blink a few times. I want to laugh, but the look on his face tells me that's a very bad idea. "Johns Hopkins?" I practically squeak. "What happened?"

"What do you mean, what happened?"

My goodness, he sounds tetchy.

"I mean... why didn't you go?"

He shrugs. "I bought the bar."

"You chose this bar"—I point down at the wooden bar top—"over medical school at *Johns Hopkins?*"

"Yeah."

"Okay." I chuckle. "Interesting."

"Are you laughing at me? Judging me?"

My God. He's really angry. At *me*. "Look." I slide off my stool. "You invited me here for dinner." I stand next to my stool, pushing it closer to the bar. "This was obviously a bad idea. You're not in the mood—"

"I'm sorry," he says so quickly I almost miss it. "I... uh... get a little defensive about it."

I scoff. "*You* brought it up all braggy and stuff."

"Braggy?" He finally laughs, sort of. It's more a scoffing sound. Nodding, he adds, "You're right. I was trying to impress you with my chem skills."

"Fair enough." I stand in the same spot, not sure what to do.

A smile is back on his handsome face. "Hop back up there. Let me feed you. What sounds good?"

"Fine," I sigh. Pulling the chair back out, I slide onto the stool. "Fried pickles, please."

He blinks a few times. "What else?"

Shaking my head, I smile back. "Nothing else."

"You have to eat more than that."

"No, that's all I want. Oh, and a diet soda."

Shaking his head, he crosses his arms highlighting his broad chest. "You need protein."

No, I really don't. "No, Luke—"

"Fine," he huffs. "Fried pickles—" He mumbles something I can't quite hear. "—coming right up."

Why do I have a feeling I'm getting more than the pickles?

~

"HERE YOU GO." Luke places a basket of deep-fried pickles onto the bar. He even includes the side of ranch dressing that's an absolute necessity. Next to that he places the biggest burger I've ever seen. "Protein."

I should be angry that he's forcing food on me, but I can't be. Instead, I look up and laugh. "I'll never be able to eat all that." I point down to what looks to be a triple-stacked burger. The truth is, I don't care for stacked meat. I know, it's a weird thing to dislike, but it is what it is. I lift the bun and see there's bacon too. Ick. *More stacked meat.*

I should just tell him.

I attempt a sympathetic look because he's about to get his feelings hurt. I can tell. "Um, I don't like it when meat is stacked on top of meat."

"Huh?" He leans closer to me. "What'd you say?"

Feeling a little self-conscious, I repeat, "I don't care for stacked meat."

"Stacked meat?" Luke looks seriously confused.

"You know." I lift the top off the burger again. "Like here." I point to the bacon. "Bacon on top of beef on top of more beef on top of...."

"More beef," he says, finishing my thought.

"Yeah."

"No stacked meat. Got it." Luke grabs the basket, pulls out the trash can, and tosses the contents inside.

"Luke!" I practically shout. "That's such a waste."

"You don't like stacked shit. I got rid of it." He stomps back to the kitchen, and I don't see him again for ten minutes. When he returns, he's got another basket in his hand. Plopping it down in front of me, he snaps, "Here."

I look down at another, much smaller burger. Lifting the bun, I see one patty and yellow cheese on top. On the side? Lettuce, tomato, and pickles. "Better?"

"Luke...."

"What's wrong with that one?" He points at the cheeseburger. I don't dare say a word. "Nothing." I smile. "Ketchup?"

"Sure." He steps back through the kitchen doors and in moments, he's back with every condiment possible.

"Thanks." I smile up at him as I squirt ketchup on the cheeseburger I didn't want, add the lettuce and other sides, put the bun back on, and then lift it and bite. "Mm," I say honestly. Chewing, I nod a couple of times. My mouth is full, but I think he's waiting for something from me. "Good." And it is. It's really good. So good, I eat the entire thing. I even get through half the fried pickles.

Finishing up, I pull out my wallet. "How much—"

"No," he snaps. "I invited you here to eat dinner."

"Oh." I don't dare argue with the man. He's quite indignant when you disagree with him. Instead, I smile up at him. "Thank you."

I watch his shoulders relax. "Good. You're welcome."

As I get ready to leave, I thank him again. When his back is turned, I set a ten-dollar bill down beneath my glass. What? It's a tip. "See you... uh... later."

"Yep," he says as he helps someone at the bar. I guess he's done talking.

Out on the sidewalk, I look right, trying to remember where I parked my car. When it comes back to me, I turn left and head down to Lincolnway. That's when I hear "Tayler."

Turning back, I see Luke jogging toward me. "Here." He's holding out the money I left.

I smile wide. "That's a tip."

Luke doesn't speak, just glares, so I reach out and take the money from his hand. "It's customary to leave a tip," I mumble.

"My friends don't tip me."

Oh, so now we're friends? That's interesting. Could have fooled me.

I'm instantly angry. "You know what, Luke?" I say his name so succinctly, I spit a little bit on the *k* sound. I don't wait for him to answer. I also shove the money back at him. "I can leave you a fucking tip if I want to. You're not the boss of me, Luke Green." Nobody is. "And you can knock off all that grumpy bullshit while you're at it. If we're"—I point to him, then myself, then use air quotes—"going to be 'friends,' then you're going to have to be a whole lot nicer to me. If anyone gets to be surly, it's me." I point to myself. "Got it?"

Luke starts to say something, but I interrupt. "And if all I want to eat is fried fucking pickles, then that's all I want to eat. I appreciate you thinking you know what's best for me, but you don't. I watch what I eat. I exercise." Mostly. "I don't need you guilting me into eating more food." Dylan used to tell me what to eat. I ate whatever *he* wanted to eat, never what *I* wanted. It pissed me off then too. A lot.

"Okay," Luke says softly. "I'm sorry."

He's sorry? I bet that was painful for him to say. He doesn't seem like the kind of guy who apologizes too much.

I take in a deep breath. "Fine." I nod. "Good." We understand one another.

"Just don't tip me."

I roll my eyes hard. "Fine." I reach out and grab the ten bucks. I'm broke right now, so I could use the money. "Bye, Luke."

"Bye, babe."

Babe? Ugh.

Friends. He wants to be friends. I roll my eyes again. I know one thing for certain, being Luke Green's friend is not going to be easy.

CHAPTER FIVE

Luke

What the hell am I doing?

I look back over my shoulder at the departing Tayler "Forever Girl" Sorensen and stare.

When I glimpse her round little ass, I remember what I'm doing.

Holy shit, the woman is wearing some of those tight-as-fuck legging things, some short little sweatshirt top, and sneakers. The sight makes my dick hard on the spot. I didn't see her enter the bar because; I was busy in the back. Same when she left. I was helping a customer, so this is the first look I've gotten of her clothes. Of her body *in* her clothes, and hot damn, she's got a great little bottom and strong thighs for such a slight thing. She can't be more than five-three and can't weigh more than a buck twenty.

She's so different than the kind of woman I typically go for. Ordinarily, I'm attracted to tall, leggy blondes. Tayler is short and a little thick on the bottom. Plus, she's got that hair. It's red as fuck, like fire, and it's long, although I've only seen it down once, maybe twice. She usually has it in a ponytail or in one of those silly buns the girls wear nowadays. They look good on her, though. Like a sexy librarian.

Ooh, Tayler Sorenson in a pencil skirt and some thick-rimmed glasses with one of those buns.

Fuck. Stop with the fantasies. I've got shit to do in the bar, and I can't have a hard-on at work.

I watch her turn the corner and out of sight. Part of me feels a little sad that I can't see her anymore, but the other part, the smarter part, thinks it's a damn good idea she's out of my sight. Any more time spent with the girl is going to test my resolve. She's something else. She's got moxie, spirit. On anyone else, it'd piss me off. Hell, if anyone tried to talk to me like she just did, I'd probably ban them from the bar for life. Not her, though. Nope. I liked watching Tayler say her piece. Either way, seeing how much backbone the woman has is a turn-on. It makes me wonder what she'd be like in bed.

Hell. Everything about her makes me wonder that. I guess I should knock that off because we're friends now.

Just friends.

Forever Girl: Hey, "friend".

She put friend in quotes. Funny. I already hate this. Well, at least she wrote first. There's that. Too bad it's two in the morning. I just got home from the bar and she's still up?

Me: Yeah?

Forever Girl: Chemistry question.

Me: Sure.

Forever Girl: How in the eff did you major in this shit? It sucks.

Me: It came easy to me.

Forever Girl: Not to me.

Me: What's your major?

Forever Girl: Interior Dsn and Mktg

I know what that is. Interior design and marketing. Strange combination.

Me: What're you going to do with that? Sell curtains?

Forever Girl: ...

No reply for a bit. So, I try again.

Me: Just kidding.

Forever Girl: I want to work at a design firm. The marketing degree is my safety net.

She's got a safety net degree?

Me: Which design firm?

There aren't that many.

Me: Doing what specifically?

Forever Girl: Designing commercial interiors. I don't know where.

Me: Good plan.

Forever Girl: Never mind. Night.

Me: I didn't mean that the way it sounded.

But she doesn't respond. Not that night. Not for a bunch of them.

Not until I text *her*.

CHAPTER SIX

Tayler

He was making fun of me. That's sort of a red flag for me. No, not "sort of." It *is* a red flag. I grew up with a house full of know-it-all men. They always thought they knew better than me like my judgement was somehow flawed mainly because I was the only girl and the baby of the family. The fact that I looked just like my mom wasn't in my favor either since she ran off with her boss, Mr. Jenson, when I was fourteen and never came back. Because of all that, it felt like I was suffocating at times. When I left for college, it was the best thing that ever happened to me. I could finally breathe.

Don't misunderstand me. I wasn't abused or anything like that. I know they love me, and it definitely got better when dad remarried my former kindergarten teacher. We were all happier when that happened and I consider her much more of a mother than the one that gave birth to me because she loves my dad and she loves us. In retrospect, dad's better off. We all are.

I release a heavy sigh after thinking about my family. I need to talk to Quinn. She'll give me feedback. I drag my phone out of my purse.

Me: Your boss is very complicated.

Quinn: **snort** Is that code for he's an asshole?

Me: LOL. Pretty much.

Quinn: When did you see him?

Me: Last night. He invited me to Cy's so he could feed me dinner.

Quinn: Serious?

Me: Serious.

Quinn: What'd you order?

Me: Fried pickles.

Quinn: Shocker. You love those stupid things.

Me: I do. But he thought it "wasn't enough protein" so he cooked me a triple bacon cheeseburger too.

Quinn: Uh-oh. Did you talk to him about your strange aversion to stacked meat?

Me: Yep. Had to nip that shit in the bud. {{shiver}}

Quinn: No doubt. So...

Me: So, then I sent him a text later that night, you know, because I was up late...

Quinn: Of course you were. Kind of like now. It's after 1am.

I stay up late. Sue me.

Me: Anyhoo, he sort of insulted my major and future career.

Quinn: And? What'd you do?

Me: I quit texting. He apologized, but I was over it by then.

Me: Oh, and he called me "babe." But that was earlier.

Quinn: What does it mean? Are you considering taking him up on his offer?

Me: If I did, it'd probably be the best sex of my life.

Quinn: Mm hmm. But you don't do that.

Me: Maybe I should.

Quinn: For Luke Green? He's hot, but is he worth you doing something completely out of character?

Me: He's not just hot. He's smokin' hot, grrrl.

God, his tattoos would make any girl swoon, but add that to his body.... He must work out every single day. He's got beautiful, sleek muscles, but he's not all huge and roided out. At least he doesn't look that way. It's not his clothes either, because I've only ever seen him in tees and jeans. It's the way they fit him like a glove. Can you tell I've spent a good amount of time checking him out? It's true. Even when I was with Dylan. And why not? Dylan used to check out girls all the time. He'd joke about it and say nobody was as hot as me. I was stupid enough to believe him. So, what did it hurt if I noticed someone like Luke? He was out of my league anyway. Not to mention I never would have cheated on Dylan. I thought it was the same for him.

Quinn: OMG. You're crazy. Grrrl? LOL

Me: I'm sleep-deprived. Forgive me.

Quinn: No need to forgive. Luke is quite a looker. Too bad he's so cranky all the time.

Cranky *and* hot is a lethal combination—as long as it's not directed at me.

Me: Going to bed. Love you, Q.

Quinn: Me too. <3. Night, lovey.

Me: Night.

∾

I SMILE AT MY PHONE. I'm so happy Quinn and I are back to normal. Heck, I think things are stronger than ever now. It's weird how friendships like ours can last so long and endure things like fights that last weeks and come out stronger on the other side. I know Quinn and I will always be tight. We'll be there for each other through thick and thin. The reason I know this is because I made a promise to myself that day at the Hub. The day Cooke surprised her. I wasn't going to judge her anymore. Yeah, I know you're probably laughing your ass off at that statement, but I mean it. She's a grown-ass woman. She can love whomever she wants. My job is to be there if and when it all falls apart. I'll be there with a bottle of wine and a voodoo doll of the asshole, whoever he is.

Quinn has never judged me. Well, okay, I had one boyfriend she hated. The one before Dylan. Quinn was right about him. His name was Kyle and *he* was an asshole. I see it now. Not at the time, though. At the time I thought he was the GOAT—greatest of all time. Turns out he was the WOAT—worst of all time. Yeah, I made that last one up. I need to trust Quinn more than I have in the past. And I will. Promise.

Setting my phone down on my nightstand, I snuggle beneath my covers. October in Iowa is unpredictable weather-wise. It can be downright hot or there could be snow on the ground. Right now, it's getting chillier by the day. I've been putting off using the furnace in the apartment because I don't need another bill right now. I look around my room and frown at the boxes stacked along the wall and it reminds me— I need to move soon. When Dylan left—or I guess I should say when I kicked him out—he left a ton of his shit here. Half of the packed boxes are his, and the rest are mine.

"God." I sigh. Where the hell will I go?

Getting comfortable, I close my eyes and do my best to force myself to sleep. Sleep hasn't been my friend of late. I'm surprisingly well on my way when I hear a knock on my door. I blink my eyes open and look at my clock. One forty-five. I can only guess who it is. I could ignore it, but then he might wake the neighbors, and I don't want to get them involved. They already hate Dylan and therefore me by default.

Throwing off the covers, I hit the light switch on my way out of my bedroom. It gives me enough light to get to the front door. Peeking through the security hole, I groan. "Dylan. Go home." Wherever the hell that is. Last I heard, he was sleeping on a friend's couch. At least he's not living with *Savanna*. Ugh, what a stupid name.

"Red."

Yeah, he calls me Red. Real original, I know.

"Go. Home."

"This *is* my home."

"Not anymore."

"Come on, let me in. Just for a minute."

He's getting louder. My guess? He's been drinking.

I groan again, then turn the deadbolt and undo the chain. Pulling the door open, I step aside. "You've got five minutes to say whatever the fuck you need to say, and then you need to leave."

"Jesus," he mutters. "You're such a bitch."

That makes the hair on my arms stand up. It also makes my eyes burn. "I'm—" I clear my throat. "I'm not a bitch." *You fucking asshole.*

"Red." He turns to face me, then scans me from head to toe. I'm wearing baggy pajamas, thankfully, but that doesn't seem to stop him from practically leering at me. "You look good."

I do not look good. I know my hair is a mess, I haven't slept much in weeks, and I'm depressed. So no, I look like shit.

"What do you want? Did you come to get your shit?" I point to the boxes stacked around the room.

He finally notices. "You packed my stuff?"

I nod. I did. I bought boxes and bubble wrap from the UPS store and packed up his stuff. I even took the time to bubble wrap his precious MLB bobblehead figures. He's got a million of them, and I swear they're his most prized possession. I should have just tossed them into a box and not done the nice thing to protect them, but I'm not like that.

When he sees a box I've labeled for him: Dylan's stupid fucking bobbleheads, he mumbles and steps closer to the cardboard cube, "My bobbleheads,"

"Yep. You should take that with you when you go." *Along with the rest of your stuff.*

He turns to look at me. "I don't have a place yet."

I shrug. I don't care. "Better find one. I'm moving soon, and I'm not taking that with me." I point to some boxes of his.

"Don't be hasty, Red."

Has anyone ever used a nickname on you that you hated? Well, Dylan knows I hate "Red." I've told him a gazillion times.

"We're not getting back together."

He snorts. "I know. Not right now, anyway. But we could still live together."

"It's a one-bedroom apartment."

"Don't you trust me?" he asks with a smirk.

"No. I absolutely don't trust you." *You cheated on me, you fuckhead.*

"Red." He's stepped closer to me, so I step back. "I need a place to live. You can't afford this place on your own. It makes perfect sense." He's stopped moving now that he's less than a foot away from me. I can't move anymore thanks to the front door at my back.

"Uh, no."

"We could be roommates." He said that last part softly. I know his game. He's doing his sweet-guy routine. "It'd be fun." He shrugs. "And maybe we could work on our relationship. Fix what's broken."

"What's broken is your dick found its way inside another woman."

"Savanna is—"

I hold up my hand. "Nope. Don't speak of her and you. I don't want to hear it. It's over between us. You're not moving back in here, and we're not 'working on our relationship.'"

"Harsh, Red." He moves closer. I see his arm raise from my peripheral vision. He's going to try to touch my face. It's how he kisses. He puts both hands on either side of my face right before he kisses me. I hate it. He controls my head that way, and it pisses me off just thinking about it. Sliding to my left, I move away from him and the door. I'm able to reach the knob, though. Opening the door, I don't smile. "Not nice to see you, Dylan. You need to go."

"Red—"

"God. Stop calling me Red!" I shout it this time. "I hate it."

"You do?" He says it like he's hearing it for the first time ever when it's closer to the millionth time. He's so full of shit. How and why did I put up with his crap for four years?

"Get out, Dylan."

He chuckles as he steps over the threshold. "Think about it. I'll be back for my bobbleheads, Red...er, Ginger."

Ugh, I hate that one too. Originality is one of Dylan's strong suits.

Without another word, I slam the door shut before he can say another stupid word. "Fuck!" I say loud enough for him to hear because I don't care. I triple lock the door, then stomp back to my bedroom.

There's no way I'm going to sleep now, so I grab my computer and decide to write the paper that's not due for two weeks. "Might as well get something done."

Tomorrow, classes are going to suck having had no sleep, but there's nothing I can do about it now.

CHAPTER SEVEN

Luke

Me: You forgive me yet?

I t's been a couple of days since she last messaged me. At first, I figured it was for the best. There's no need to get all into this girl, because she and I want two different things. But in the short time I've gotten to know her, I like her. She's cool. Most of all, she doesn't put up with my bullshit.

Tayler: What's to forgive?
Me: I was being judgmental about your degree.
Tayler: That you were. No worries.
Me: Good. Glad to hear that. So, what're you doing tonight?
Tayler: Luke, I'm not going to sleep with you.
Me: Well aware, babe. Just thought you'd like to hang out at the bar tonight. It's Friday and which means you can't use the excuse of homework.
Tayler: Is Quinn working?
Me: Until 9.
Tayler: Yeah, I'll stop by.

Stop by? What does that mean? Is she going somewhere else?

Tayler: C U later.

Me: Yep. Later, babe.

CHAPTER EIGHT

Tayler

I walk into Cy's and look at the bar first. I see one of the other bartenders but no Quinn. I scan the place and see it's pretty busy. Not a surprise for a Friday night. Making my way up to said bar, I find an empty stool and climb on.

"What can I getcha, pretty lady?"

Ignoring the compliment, I say, "Diet soda, please."

"Right on," the guy says as he grabs a glass.

I lean to my right a little to see if I can spot Quinn in the kitchen area. Not there. Next, I rotate on my seat and search the bar one more time. I'm about to ask the bartender where she is when Luke appears from the back room. Without even greeting him, I ask, "Where's Quinn?" It's only seven. I came early just to hang with her.

"Uh," Luke says, then stops. He crosses his arms over his chest and stares at me. "Well...."

I blink a few times, trying to figure out why he's acting weird, then ask again. "Where's Quinn?"

"She, uh, left."

Bartender guy sets my soda down in front of me and walks

away. Fast. "She left? You let her go early?" I scan the bar and note how busy it is. "It's packed in here."

"I... well, I didn't let her go early. She got pissed and left."

I just took my first drink of soda when his words register. I nearly spit everything onto the bar. "Quinn got pissed and left?" I arch my brow at Luke. "What'd you do?" Because my girl would not leave work early unless she had a very good reason.

"Me?" he squeaks. Yes, he squeaked. "I...." He lets his arms drop to the side. Leaning closer, he whispers, "I got pissed at her and told her to move her Kardashian ass."

I gasp. Anger hits me so hard and so fast, it makes me dizzy. He has no idea. None whatsoever about what Quinn has gone through related to her body. The last thing she needs is someone like Luke making a comment like that. "You fucking asshole," I growl.

"I know—"

"No you don't, fuckwit."

"Come on. It's a compliment."

No. He. Didn't. "Telling a woman she's got a big ass is a compliment?"

"Yes. Every woman wants a big ass."

"No. Not every woman wants a big ass, you moron." My voice is getting louder. "Someone who's had to watch her weight her entire life isn't happy to have a big ass, *Luke*."

He runs his fingers through his dirty-blond hair. I can't help noticing how pink his face has gotten. "Fine!" he says loudly. "I fucked up!"

"Yeah, you did. You hurt my b-best friend." I'm tearing up now. No man is worth this shit. Sliding off the stool, I grab my purse and head to the door. I'm not spending another minute with this guy.

"Tayler!" he shouts as I walk through the door into the chilly night. Ignoring him, I stop and look right, thinking about where I parked a mere ten minutes ago. Gah! Stupid Luke has my brain fizzling. When I hear the door to Cy's open and my name being called again, I start walking. I'm halfway up the street when I remember I need to go the other way. No matter, I'm not turning back. I'll just walk around the block. I need the exercise anyway.

I feel someone touch my shoulder, and I know it's him. "Babe."

Wiping away a tear or two, I turn to face him. "What?" I shout.

"Look. I'm sorry. I'm an asshole."

"Yeah?" Tell me something I don't know.

"I'll apologize to her. I'll kiss her... uh, I'll make sure she knows how sorry I am."

"You'd better not fire her."

"Fire her?" He stops talking for a second. "No, she's not fired. Why would she be fired?"

"Because she left."

"I don't blame her. I was out of line."

I nod because I don't know what to say to that. "You don't know Quinn. If you did, you'd never say something shitty like that to her again. She's the kindest, most loyal—" I get choked up again. "Don't treat her like you do everyone else."

He stares at me for a second. Then he reaches out and moves the hair that fell out of my bun away from my face. Using his thumb, he wipes away one of my tears. "I'm sorry, honey." His voice is so soft, I barely hear him. "No, I don't know Quinn very well, but I do know she's special. I knew the second the words left my mouth it hurt her. But I was proud of her. She stood up for herself. She let me have it." He chuckles. "She has balls."

I like what he said, but I'm still not happy with him. "Don't do it again."

His hand drops from my cheek, and it makes me a little sad. I hate to admit, I like the warmth. "I'll try."

I'm not sure trying is enough, to be honest. Dylan tried not to cheat on me, and look where that got us. This seems like it'd be a no-brainer, but maybe it's too hard for Luke. So I tell him, "You'll *try* not to be a jerk to the sweetest girl on the planet?"

With a chuckle, he remarks, "Who we talkin' about now? You or Quinn?"

I roll my eyes. "Quinn." I'm not sweet. I'm sour.

"DID you make him not fire me?" Quinn asks with an arched brow.

I'm driving my best friend home from the hospital after she was run off the road on her scooter. She called me from the ER and asked if I could pick her up. Duh. God, I was so scared when she called to tell me what had happened. I did my best to remain calm on the phone with her, but I let that shit out on the ride to the hospital.

"No. He said he was an asshole and that he was proud that you stuck up for yourself."

"Before I left, I told him I was going to tell on him... to you." She giggles, then winces.

My poor bestie is in pain. "Well, he beat you to it."

"So, what's wrong?"

"Dylan." I roll my eyes, but she can't see me because it's dark in the car. "He wants me back."

"Of course he does. But you're not taking him back, right?" The car is silent while I think about it. "Tay?"

No, I'm not taking him back, but I'm still sad. "We were together for so long."

"And?"

"He's—"

"A cheating bastard. Besides, what about Luke?"

"Luke has his head up his ass."

"How so?"

"He can't see past just hooking up. I mean, I should probably go along with it, since I was in a serious relationship for so long. I *should* have some fun. Honestly, things with me and Dylan have been over a long time. We just drifted apart when we got up here to Ames, but neither one of us did anything about it."

I hear a snort from Quinn. "Dylan did something about it."

"True." We drive in silence for a few minutes. "No."

"No what?"

"No, I'm not taking Dylan back. I'm also not going to be some guy's hookup. There are plenty of girls who want that. I'm just not one of them."

"And you told Luke all of that?"

"Pretty much. I don't think we want the same thing." She shrugs. "I get it."

"I'm sorry, Tay-Tay."

Yeah, I don't care for that nickname either, but it's okay coming from Quinn. I know she means it as a term of endearment.

I glance over, giving Quinn a weak smile. "So, you were nearly run over, huh?"

"Oh, well, that was the good part of my day. The rest really sucked."

Now that makes me laugh. Hard.

We decide it's best if she just crashes—no pun intended—at my place for tonight. She already sent a text to her roommates letting them know she was staying with me.

When we pull into my apartment complex, she frowns. "You've got stairs."

She's wearing a boot on her foot and limping a lot. Stairs would suck. "There's a service elevator. We'll use that."

"Thank goodness."

I wrap my arm around her waist and lead her through the door to the back of the main level. I press the button and wait as the elevator clanks and wheezes its way down to us.

"So, where did they take your scooter?"

"Gage took care of it."

"He's a nice guy."

"He is." She sighs.

I give her a side-eye. "Plus he's got a thing for you." At my door, I unlock the deadbolt and push the door open.

Quinn ignores my comment and changes the subject as she steps into my place. "You're ready to move? Did you find a place yet?" Quinn sounds a little surprised.

"Most of that is Dylan's stuff. He thinks he's just going to move back in here, but I took care of that. I've started packing my stuff too." I shrug. "Why not? I've got to be out of here. Our lease is up on the fifteenth."

Quinn has a funny expression on her face.

"Yeah. Dylan wanted to be in before Thanksgiving last year, so he talked the management into a midmonth move-in date." I roll my eyes, then mutter, "Idiot."

I'm surprised by Quinn's next words. "I think I need to move too."

"Really? Why?"

Sitting down on my sofa, she puts her bad foot up on my ancient coffee table and begins to tell me about her current living situation since the basement of her rental flooded and the subsequent mold that grew because of standing water. Then there was the story of her ineffective landlord.

"And then there's the spider," she says with a shiver.

God, even if the landlord did fix up the basement... "Would you want to live there knowing there's probably a million baby spiders running around? Spiders can lay like two hundred eggs at a time."

"Great." Quinn laughs. "Thanks for that." She rubs her face with both of her hands. "Now I'm just picturing a basement full of Aragogs."

"Well, that's just crazy," I growl. "Why won't the landlord do more?"

"Patsy threatened him so he just sort of shut down on us."

"God, I hate landlords like that. So spiteful."

Quinn adds after a yawn, "It is the way it is."

"Oh, girl. You're tired." I jump up and I head to my hall closet to gather up a sheet, blanket, and pillow for Quinn. As I make up her bed, she pulls off her torn-up sweatshirt.

"There, lie down. You hungry? Thirsty?" I ask as I make my way to my kitchen.

"I'd take some water. I need to take one of these pain pills."

"Sure."

I pull a glass down from my cupboard and search for some crackers. When I find what I'm looking for, I head back to the couch and set both on the coffee table. "You need to eat something with those things."

"Thanks, Tay."

"No problem."

I watch her take her pain pill and nibble on a cracker. It's then that it hits me. She could have been killed tonight. I sniffle because it can't be helped.

She jerks her head up to look at me. "What's wrong?"

"You could have been killed." I'm blubbering now.

"I wasn't."

"Fucking scooters," I snap.

"It wasn't Bluebell's fault. It was the idiot driver of the SUV."

Wiping my eyes, I can't help scowling. "You know what I mean. You're my best friend. I don't want to lose you."

"I'm right here. I'm fine."

"I know." My voice is so soft. The words are hard to say. "You should call your boyfriend and tell him you're okay."

"He's... not. This morning...." She can't seem to finish.

"Jesus, you did have a bad day, didn't you?"

"Told you."

I run my palm over her hair. "Poor Q." Sitting on the coffee table in front of her, I smile because I've got a great idea. "We should totally live together."

"You think?" Quinn seems surprised by my suggestion.

I nod quickly. "Absolutely. We'd have a blast."

"We would." She holds her good hand out to me for a shake. "Roomies."

I place my hand in hers. "Roomies." Thank goodness. "All right. I'm going to head to bed." I stand and walk in the direction of my room when I hear Quinn laugh. Turning back, I ask, "What?"

"Luke texted."

I cross my arms over my chest and arch a brow. This better be good.

Quinn reads, "**Luke:** I'm sorry. I was an ass. I deserved that. Don't quit. You're a good bartender." She laughs. "**Luke:** Having a Kardashian ass isn't an insult, by the way. People pay thousands of dollars for that ass. You got it for free (I assume)."

I watch as Quinn types. "What're you saying back?"

She snickers as she reads aloud. "**Me:** My ass was homegrown, *thankyouverymuch*. I won't quit, but I was run off the road tonight, and I'm pretty beat up and now wearing a boot, so we'll have to talk about it when I can come back."

I smile at her words. Luke was right, she's got balls. Well, lady balls.

"**Me:** And by the way... WTF are you doing with Tayler? She's not a booty call kind of girl. She's the forever kind."

I gasp at her last text. "Quinn."

"Wait, he just replied. **Luke**: I know."

If he knows, then what is he doing? Gah! Men are so frustrating. Especially Luke Green.

CHAPTER NINE

Luke

I've been down a bartender for almost a week due to Quinn's accident. I found out more about what happened last night from one of her chatty roommates. It sounds like she dodged a bullet. It could have been much worse. Even so, I've checked on Quinn a couple of times plus it gave me an excuse to talk to Tayler.

What? I'm not a monster. But, I guess it makes me an opportunist. Sue me. She forgave me after I promised I'd "never say a disparaging word against Quinn Maxwell again." I *will* keep my damn word. It's bad enough to have one strong-willed woman (Quinn) pissed at me, but two? No thanks.

I'm off work for once. I took two days off *in a row* to do some work to my house. I've neglected this property for the other one, my bar, for far too long. But a couple of days is just what I need to replace the faucet in the kitchen and take a look at the roof to see if I can just patch it or have to replace the whole damn thing. I'm rooting for the patch job. I'd also like to paint my bedroom. It's been the same deep red color since I bought the place a couple of years ago, and I'm sick of it. Sleeping in a red room gives me the creeps. It's probably why I crash on the couch most nights.

The surprising part of all of this—and the reason I'm blabbering on about it—is Tayler offered to help me paint. I don't need an interior designer, but I sure could use Tayler's company. Not only that, it'll be the first time she'll see my place. I hope she likes it.

When a knock sounds on my front door, a zing of nerves hits me. *She's here.* When she knocks again, I yell, "Coming!" so she doesn't take off.

Opening the old door, I smile at the sight of her in a pair of bib overalls over what looks like an old T-shirt. She's got her hair in two braids on either side of her pretty face. Front and center to all that is her smile. She's fucking gorgeous. "Designer extraordinaire at your service," she chirps.

Pushing open the screen door, when she passes close to me I smell her scent. It's good. Pretty. Like flowers. "Welcome," I say after I take a deep swallow.

"Wow," she says, turning in a circle in my living room. "Craftsman, huh?"

"Yep."

"Please tell me there are built-ins in the dining room."

"There's one large one." She wasn't lying. She's into this. "Someone painted it a long time ago, though. I've been meaning to strip it down to match the rest of the woodwork." I mean, who paints wood like that?

"Good plan," she says like she really does know. "It's a damn shame when people do stuff like that. It was stained for a reason." She's got her hands on her little hips, looking rather fierce. It's downright adorable.

I chuckle softly, then smile. I like her here. She's so damn cute in her painting outfit. And there's just something about her in my house that feels right.

"I'll show you." I point to the open doorway in the wall. She goes first and steps into my dining room slash office. "See?"

"Oh my God. It's orange."

I nod and point to the floor. "Yep. It matches the linoleum."

"I bet there are hardwoods under this."

"Yeah, I pulled up one of the tiles and there are."

"This place could be amazing," she says with a breathy voice.

"That's why I bought it."

"Show me to the bedroom." She blushes.

I'd love to show her my bed... room.

I smile to myself as I lead us back to the living room and down a short hallway. "Here's where the magic happens." When she blushes again, I wrap her up in my arms and bring her to my chest. I'm laughing now. So hard my body is shaking.

"Jerk," she mutters into my shirt.

When I stop laughing, I let her go. "I hate this red color. I can't sleep in here."

"Redrum, redrum," she says in a husky voice.

"Ah, *The Shining*. Great movie."

She's still right up against me, so when she looks up and says, "I've never seen it," all I can see are her pretty eyes and her lashes as she blinks.

"Well, then we *have* to watch it."

"But first, we need to paint this room. What color did you get?"

"Blue."

"Oh, blue is perfect. It's great to sleep in a room painted a cool color."

"Hm, I just like blue, so I got blue."

She giggles. "That works too." Tayler claps her hands. "It looks like you did all the hard work. Everything is all taped off, you've got a drop cloth, and the furniture is mostly gone. Let's get started."

I put on some old Beatles vinyl—lady's choice—and we paint. It takes so many coats that I have to run to the hardware store for more paint.

"We should have primed," Tayler says, plopping her pretty ass down on my couch. "Red is really hard to cover."

"I had no idea." I really didn't. "Four coats of paint. It looks good, though."

"It does." She's smiling at me, and I'm smiling right back. I had fun doing a task I really dreaded doing. "You should help me paint this living room."

She flops her head back, looking at the dark tan-hued walls. "Sure. I just need a day or two to recover." Looking over at me, she smirks. "You gonna let me pick the color?"

"Sure. Just no red." It makes her laugh, and I fucking love the sound.

"So, pizza and *The Shining*?"

Tayler pulls her phone from the little pocket on the bib of her overalls and presses some buttons. Shrugging, she says, "Sure."

Honestly, I'm surprised she doesn't have to run off and study. It is Sunday, after all. Of course, I'm not about to mention any of that. I want her to stay a while longer. "What kind of pizza?"

Please say pepperoni.

"Pepperoni and mushroom?"

"Sweet." I can pick off the shrooms. "I'll order from Jeff's. They deliver."

"Ooh, in that case, can we get the spinach, Havarti, and artichoke pizza?"

No. "Sure." I smile, but I'm not doing it convincingly.

"No." She snorts. "I can tell by your face that you don't like that."

"How 'bout half that and half pepperoni?"

"Sure. That's fair."

I order the food and am tempted to jump into the shower, but that's not polite. She's still in her painting gear. "You want to shower?" I ask because I'm a gentleman like that.

"Um." She looks at me. "Sure. I've got a change of clothes in my car."

She does? "You do?"

"Workout stuff."

Oh Jesus. It's probably some of those tight-ass legging things.

"Ladies first. You shower and I'll cue up the movie."

"Sounds good." Tayler moves from the couch much slower than earlier today. Painting is hard work. My body is sore, and I do physical shit all day every day.

I search my shelf for the DVD of our movie. Sure, it's probably on one of those subscription services, but I don't have those. Why would I? I'm never home, and there's no time to watch shit at work.

By the time I find the movie on the bottom shelf, Tayler is already out of the shower. She's got her paint clothes rolled up into a ball in her hand, and her hair is still in the same braids, so she must not have washed her hair, but the adorable dabs of paint that used to be on her nose and cheek are now gone, sadly. Not only that, she's dressed in exactly what I feared—tight gray legging things and a tiny top.

"Jesus." I mutter to myself. This is going to be a long night.

I jump up and set the movie on the coffee table. "Money for the pizza is on the table next to the door. Be right back."

I walk quickly to my spare room, where my clothes are currently stashed until I can put my room back together. I need some briefs made of steel, because seeing her in that tiny outfit has made my dick stiff. Finding a pair of compression shorts, I grab those, some clean sweats, and a tee.

I make quick work of the shower, so I'm dry and dressed in only a few minutes. I adjust my cock in the tight compression shorts and wince a little bit. I hate wearing shit like this. I'd rather let the boys fly free, but it's for the best. I want Tayler to come back.

"Pizza's here," her pretty voice says from the other room. When I step into the room, she's setting out two plates, a couple of paper towels, and forks. "I got us some beers from your fridge." She stands up to full height. "I hope that's okay."

"Sure." Normally I'd probably balk at someone going through my shit, but it doesn't bother me which surprises me a little bit. "Smells good."

"It does. They sent breadsticks too."

"Sunday special."

"Yum."

Tayler and I sit at the same time. Handing me a plate, she opens up the pizza box. "I love Jeff."

I jerk my head over to look at her, wondering who the fuck Jeff is. Then, I remember.... It's just the name of the pizza joint.

"It's okay." I'm lying, I love Jeff's pizza too.

Ignoring me, Tayler grabs the biggest slice of the artichoke side of the pizza and bites into it. I smile watching her as she devours her slice. She stops eating and points to the box. "Aren't you going to eat?"

"Yep." Grabbing two slices and several breadsticks, I lean back on my sofa. It's my favorite piece of furniture. I've had it for years, and I intend to keep it forever. It's deep and so comfortable I can't imagine my life without it.

When Tayler slides back after taking a second slice, I snicker. Like I said, the couch is deep. So deep her feet no longer touch the floor.

"Don't laugh at my stubby legs, Mr. Green."

Placing my palm over my chest, I act affronted. "Never, shorty."

"Whatever." She rolls her eyes. "Are we gonna watch the movie or what?"

I set my plate down and do her bidding. Hitting Play, I sit back down, this time just a little closer to my... to Tayler.

"The music is ominous already." I half expect her to laugh, but she doesn't. What she does do is scoot just a little closer to me. *Note to self: get more scary movies.*

"You don't like scary movies?"

"Is this scary?" she squeaks.

"I'd say it was more suspenseful." And scary.

"Oh geez," she grumbles. "I don't know about this."

Chuckling, I pull on one of her pretty braids. "You're the one who said 'redrum, redrum.'" I do my best to mimic the creepy voice from the movie.

"Yeah, but I didn't know what it meant."

"It's murder spelled backward."

"Oh my God." She drops her half-eaten slice back onto the plate and turns to look at me. "I don't know about this."

Reaching out, I pull her closer to me. "No worries. I'll protect you." Then I do the weirdest thing: I kiss the top of her head. I should pull away. I should apologize, but I can't figure out how to do it without making me seem like a fucking tool. So, keeping my arm just where it was, I reach down with my right hand and pick up my pizza and eat. I'll just do that all one-handed.

Grumbling, Tayler says, "This is a bad idea," then takes a bite of her food.

On the contrary, this is a great idea. Maybe the best idea I've ever had.

CHAPTER TEN

Tayler

Disoriented. That's what I am. Disoriented but surprisingly comfortable.

I blink my eyes open and lift my head, attempting to get my bearings. Oh, I'm at Luke's. Not only that, I'm *on* Luke. Well, almost. My head was on his chest and my hand somehow found its way under his tee. It's resting on top of a hard stomach. I can literally feel muscle. I'm tempted to run my hand over the rest of his bare abdomen, but that's a terrible idea. Not only that, his hand is firmly planted on my ass. At least it's on the outside of my yoga leggings.

I look left to the big window to gauge the time, but the old curtains are drawn. No matter the time, I need to get up, get home, and prepare for class. I've got a test this morning.

I roll to my left, attempting to get my feet beneath me, and lose my balance, landing on my back on the floor between the couch and the coffee table. The urge to laugh at my predicament hits me, but I do my best to hold it in. I don't want to wake him up.

As I'm about to push myself up, a messy blond head appears above me. Messy blond hair and sleepy eyes. "Fall down, babe?"

"Well, I was trying not to wake you up."

"Stealth isn't your thing, apparently." His laugh is husky sounding like pure sex.

"Shut up," I grumble. I'm not a morning person. Especially not before coffee. "I need to go."

"It's three in the morning."

Oh.

"Come back up. I set my phone to go off at five."

"You did?" Wow, that was really sweet of him. I know for a fact that he isn't working tomorrow—er, today.

"Come on." He pats the spot next to him on the couch. "I need my beauty sleep."

No he doesn't. The man is way too beautiful as is. He's testing my resolve. The truth is, besides his hand on my butt this morning, he's been a complete gentleman. At one point in the movie, I half expected him to push me onto my back and ravage me, but he didn't. He stayed close and kept me safe from that stupid movie. I probably only fell asleep because the couch was so dang comfortable but having Luke's arm wrapped around me sure didn't help.

Staring at the empty spot on the couch, I push up to my knees. I know he won't try anything. He knows where I stand on all this. I'm not a hookup.

So, I do something I probably shouldn't. I crawl back onto the couch until I'm right back where I started, except this time, I leave my hand to rest on my own hip. My head is on his chest, as he pulls up the throw blanket until we're both covered.

"Go to sleep, honey." His voice is soft and husky, making me shiver.

Snuggling into him, I rest my hand on top of his shirt. I breathe in his clean scent. Sure, it could just be laundry detergent, but it smells a bit too musky for that. I feel his heartbeat beneath my cheek, and I smile. I could get used to this. I won't, but I could.

Taking in a deep breath, I do my best to concentrate on sleep. When his breathing evens out, mine does too. When I feel his palm slide back down to rest on top of my ass, I know I should probably ask him to move it, but I don't because his big palm is warm and rather comforting.

Bad idea, Tayler.

TWELVE DAYS AGO, we painted his bedroom blue, and he promised me I could choose the living room color if I helped him paint again. Sadly, I've heard very little from Luke Green. Correction: I've heard nothing from him. I've seen him, though. I stopped into Cy's with Quinn and the other girls from Beedle Drive, but he barely spared me a glance. Sure, it was super busy that night, but still. I didn't bother trying to talk to him either, assuming he was either in a bad mood (shocker, I know) or worse, he was over our friendship. Part of me wishes I'd found a way to talk to him that night because all I've done since is worry and fret. And believe me, worrying and fretting isn't helping me focus on school.

That's why I'm where I am right now—wondering why he's been ghosting me. The wondering is driving me crazy and because I can't stand the unknown, I've taken it upon myself to find out:

Me: I've chosen your living room color.

I wait several hours before he responds, and no, I wasn't staring at my phone the entire time.

Half the time? Absolutely.

Luke: Yeah?

I know I should wait to respond, but I'm not like that. I hate those stupid games people play.

Me: Yep.

Five minutes later...

Luke: Are you gonna tell me?

Me: I'd rather surprise you.

Luke: You aren't buying my paint, babe.

Me: No. But I've got the color swatch.

If he doesn't take the hint and invite me to the bar or wherever he is, then this is pointless.

Luke: Come by for dinner. I promise not to feed you any stacked meat.

Me: Aw, you remembered. So sweet.

Luke: How could I forget? Weirdest fucking shit I ever heard.

Me: LOL. I'll stop by. No need to feed me.

Luke: Whatever.

God, the guy is a grouch even in a simple text message. Maybe I shouldn't stop by. Maybe I'm forcing him into something he doesn't want. Either way, I'm honestly not in the mood to deal with this. At all. As a matter of fact, now *I'm* the one who's angry.

Me: Never mind...

Luke: WTF?

Me: Yeah, never mind.

I don't need this. I've got to move in days to a place I've yet to find, I practically failed my World History test, and now having to put up with this A-hole is not something I want to deal with. I'm about to turn off my phone when it rings and Luke's name appears.

I'm stupid. I answer. "Yeah?"

"What the fuck, Tayler?"

See?

"What?" I snap right back.

"What's your problem?"

My problem? Luke Green's my problem, but I'm not about to say that. "I don't have a problem. What's *your* problem?"

"I'm busy as fuck, babe."

"Well, then, go do whatever you need to do. You called *me*, remember that." I hang up without another word, and for some stupid reason, it makes me cry. Immediately. My phone rings again, and I press the icon to ignore it. Better than that, I turn off the phone completely. I'm busy too. I need to finish packing, and then Quinn and I are going apartment hunting. God, I hope we find a place. If we don't, I'll be looking for a storage unit and living in my car.

The thought makes me cry a bit harder. Sure, I'm feeling mighty sorry for myself right now. I'm entitled to be a little sad right now. I've kept myself together, for the most part, since Dylan and I... never mind. It doesn't matter. I'm human. If you don't like it, well, you can just...suck it.

Damn. More tears.

CHAPTER ELEVEN

Tayler

"What about that place?" Quinn asks me as we leave the dirtiest, grossest apartment I've ever seen.

"It was dirty. Who knows what's lurking beneath the carpet?" I pretend to shiver. "God, disgusting."

"We have one more place left, right?" My best friend is so sweet. She's doing her best to keep the faith.

"Yeah. If this one doesn't work out, we're screwed. I'm going to have to live in my car or crash at your place." Ignoring the weird look on Quinn's face, I pull into a parking lot next to a three-story brick building. It looks like someone renovated an old school. It's promising. "Here's hoping," I mutter.

We make our way to the front door. There's a small sign telling us where to find the rental office. We step in and walk slowly down a long hallway to the door with a sign that says simply "Manager." I try the knob, but it's locked, so I knock. We wait for a minute or two, and I knock again. Yeah, I'm impatient. I'm not hopeful about this place. It looks run-down.

When we hear a growly voice say, "Hold your damn horses," my first thought is Luke. Only the voice sounds even more gruff.

The door creaks open, and an old guy in a robe and jeans snaps, "What?"

Shit. I'm not in the mood for this crap. I'm about to snap right back when, thankfully, Quinn answers, "We're here to look at an apartment."

"I called earlier," I add. "My name is Tayler."

"Tayler's a man's name."

"It's also mine, uh, *sir*." I'm aware I sound just a tad sarcastic, but you should not, I'm this close to throat-punching this guy.

"Fucking confusing if you ask me." He reaches back and pulls out some keys.

At least that's a good sign. It means the place is still available, which is also bad because that most likely means it's crap that nobody else wants.

"Top floor, girls."

We follow him to a set of wooden stairs that have seen better days. There are cracked boards, and several planks are completely missing.

"Stairs are gettin' fixed next week."

Sure they are. "Is there an elevator?" Quinn asks. The poor girl is still wearing that stupid boot. She has a hard time getting around on that thing.

"Nope. Exercise would do you good, girl."

I'm about to let the asshole have it when Quinn surprises the fuck out of me. "I exercise. Don't judge a book by its cover."

He snorts. "If I did, you'd be *War and Peace*."

Again, I want to jump into the fray, but Quinn doesn't give me time. "That's rude."

He stops moving and looks right at Quinn. "Pardon?"

I stifle the giggle that's trying to escape. She's over his bullshit too. "I said that's rude. You don't know me. You don't know one thing about me, so don't presume to say something as callous as '*War and Peace*.'" Then she says, rather mockingly, "Someone your age should have better manners than that."

"Well." He chuckles. "You're a spitfire, ain't ya?"

"Yes," my bestie deadpans.

"You're a pretty thing." Then, lowering his voice, he adds, "For a big book."

Fuck this guy. I'd like to do something, but by the time I decide that, we're at the door. "This'n needs to be cleaned up and painted."

"Oh, great," I grumble. That's code for "it's a shithole."

"It's a nice one," the old guy replies. "Lots of people want to live here."

"Uh-huh." Quinn doesn't sound convinced either.

When he turns the key, the door unlatches. When he pushes the door open, we both gasp. The place is gorgeous.

"It's beautiful," Quinn says first.

She's right. It's bright and sunny. The ceilings are high, and while they look like they need painting, it's not in terrible shape. The floors are all hardwood and in decent shape. There's a chill running down my spine.

I want this place.

The kitchen is nice—open to the rest of the place. The appliances aren't new, but they aren't olive green either. There's even a big island that faces the living space.

I *want* this place.

Quinn and I make eye contact, but neither one of us speaks. She wants it too.

I check out the bedroom and nearly choke when I see the closets. There are big windows in one of the bedrooms, making it just as sunny as the living room, while the other bedroom is a little darker. The same floors from the main room are running through the bedrooms too.

Quinn and I meet in the hallway, away from the old fart. Quinn whispers, "Amazing." All I can do is nod in agreement. "What do you think?"

I feel tears burn.

"What's wrong?" she asks, placing her hand on my arm.

"I love it. It's perfect. Right?"

"Yeah. It's perfect. The price is a steal too. I wonder what the catch is."

It has to be dealing with the old guy from downstairs. *That's* the catch. "I've been wondering the same thing. I mean, was someone murdered here? Is it haunted? Does it leak?" I look up at the ceiling and smile. "Shit. Tin ceilings." I love tin ceilings.

"I know. This place is amazing. There's *got* to be a catch."

I walk around a little more, but when I hear Quinn talking to the old guy, I step into the living room. "So." Quinn has her hands on her hips. "What's the catch?"

I want to laugh at her candor, but I stay silent. I like that she's taking the lead here.

"Catch?" He chuckles. "You sure are a spitfire."

"Uh-huh. So? Is it haunted? Is it a murder apartment? Does the neighbor have a thing for college girls?"

"The neighbor is a professor at the college. I don't think he's got any weird fetishes." He shrugs. "Who knows these days. Am I right?" He chuckles again.

"What's your name?" Quinn asks like she's gathering intel.

"Vic."

"And you manage the place?"

"I own it, hon."

"And the stairs?"

"Carpenter is coming on Monday."

"And what about utilities?"

"Included. So is cable. I've also got Wi-Fi."

"Shit," Quinn mutters. "It's too good to be true."

He chuckles again. "Sometimes something good can be true too, love."

He called her love. I so want to giggle.

"We'll take it," Quinn says suddenly. "How soon can we move in?"

"Well now, you'll need to fill out an application. I've got others interested."

"See?" Quinn sounds pissed. "I knew there was a catch."

"No catch." He leans a little closer. "You're my favorite by far, girly. I'm rootin' for ya."

With a laugh, Quinn says, "Vic, we need a place to live. Tayler's boyfriend cheated on her, so she's got to move out. I was living in a basement with a spider the size of my fist." She holds up her fist for reference. "This is the best place we've seen. We need an answer now."

"My goodness, you do remind me of my beloved Mary."

"Your wife?"

"Pitbull. She's the love of my life."

I can't take it. I move in and repeat, "We'll take it."

Quinn starts to laugh, and I can tell she's not going to stop for a bit.

"Tell you what," he says, scratching his scruffy face. "If everything checks out on your applications, it's yours. It'll take me a day or so. Then I've got to paint and clean."

"We'll do that."

Quinn jumps at the chance, and I'm glad because I nod, adding, "Yeah. We'll paint and clean."

"Interesting." Vic scratches his chin again. "I'll let you know tomorrow. Is that good enough?"

"Yes!" we say at the same time.

We follow Vic back downstairs to his gorgeous apartment. It's even nicer than the one upstairs. Hell, he's even got granite counters. While we wait, Quinn whispers, "Can you believe this place?"

I shake my head. I can't. I really can't. I see movement out of the corner of my eye. A giant dog has stepped out from one of the back rooms. I instantly freeze up. I'm scared shitless of dogs. I reach out for Quinn to pull her back when the dog trots right over to her, sits down, and wags its tail in front of her.

"You must be Mary," she says, petting the dog's head. She coos at the animal, telling her how pretty she is. I'm shocked she's not at least a little scared of the large beast. "... I think I love you too."

"You're in." Vic's voice sounds sort of scratchy. "She's n-never done that before." He clears his throat. "She's a rescue. Abused somethin' terrible. She's scared of everyone." He sniffles, and it sort of makes my eyes water.

That dog must have been through something horrendous to get that reaction from the crotchety old fool.

"But not you, spitfire. She loves you. And in my book, dogs read people way better than humans. You're in. I'll have the paint and supplies up there for you tomorrow. First and last month's rent before I give you a key. You can move in tomorrow."

I'm staring at Vic while Quinn pets Mary. "Did you hear that, girl? We're going to be neighbors." Mary barks, and Quinn laughs. She stands up and reaches out to shake the man's hand. "Thanks, Vic."

Who the hell is that girl? She's not the best friend I remember. The one scared of everything. That girl is gone. Long gone.

"My pleasure, spitfire."

When we get to the car, I turn to Quinn. "Who are you?"

"What do you mean? I'm me."

"You're much more than that."

Quinn gives me a small smile, and then it grows. "We have a home. And not just any home either. It's the coolest place I've ever seen. I can't wait to decorate."

"Which reminds me. We're going to need help moving. I doubt you and I will be able to move furniture up those stairs, especially with your boot."

"My boot can come off any time. I'm just nervous about it." She pauses. "I could call the rugby guys."

"Perfect." I can't believe I'm offering this up since I'm pissed at him, but he owes me. "I'll also ask Luke if he knows anyone."

"Luke?" Quinn looks confused. "I thought...."

"We're friends. Nothing more. We talk. That's all." Sad but true.

"Good. We have a plan. Let me know what Luke says."

Yes, we sure do. Now all I have to do is execute mine.

IN THE END, I didn't get in touch with Luke. I told Quinn he was busy, and she had no reason to doubt me. Luke is always busy. Truth is, I wasn't ready to reach out to him only a day after our phone fight. No matter, the ISU rugby guys came through big-time. They made quick work of moving our things, which meant we had a lot of unpacking to do. But Quinn's part of that is now on hold. While we were moving in, Dan and Bull told Quinn about an injury Cooke sustained while playing a big rugby game. My friend was really upset. So much so, she booked a flight to England on the spot. I spent the next couple of days shuttling her home to get her passport and approval from her parents, then down to Des Moines to the airport.

Since then, I've spent the last few days alone in our new place. It sucks because I'm tired of being alone. Really tired.

CHAPTER TWELVE

Luke

What happened to my life?

I used to be so content. Okay, that's not true. Content isn't the kind of word I'd ever use to describe any part of my world. But I had a routine. One I liked. I got up, ate something, and then I came to work. Repeat. Over and over and over again.

Now that routine is making me goddamn crazy because instead of getting on with my day, I wake up and wonder if today's the day Tayler decides to call me.

Don't look at me like that.

I *have* tried to call her. It goes straight to voice mail. Well, now it does. For a while it'd ring once or twice and that's it. I know that means she declined my call. At least now she doesn't bother to do that. That's got to be an improvement, yeah?

My thoughts turn to the beautiful redhead all day long—not just first thing in the morning. It happens at lunch, at dinner, and it's especially bad at night, in my bed. I lie there in my new blue room wondering what she's doing. Part of me is worried she's with someone else, but I know that's not her style, and for once, it makes me feel at ease. I guess she could have gotten back with her ex, but Quinn didn't think that was going to happen. I hope she's right.

I know they moved last weekend. I could have taken time off to help, but according to Dan, the rugby guy, they got it all done in no time. I was pissed at first. I mean, it's a man's job to help his girl move.

Don't say it.

She's not my girl, but she is my friend. Okay, she used to be my friend. My bad attitude got in the way again. If she'd given me a chance that night, I could have told her that my beer delivery was all fucked up, which caused a chain reaction of bad shit at the bar, but I don't think it'd matter. She told me, point-blank, to quit being a "grumpy asshole". (Okay, not her exact words but that's it in a nutshell.)

I guess I didn't listen.

In my defense, though, sometimes life sucks and a guy is entitled to be an asshole. Right? Life isn't all sunshine and unicorn shit flying around. Sometimes it's bullshit.

I sigh and run my fingers through my hair. I need a cut; it's getting unruly. I also need to see her. I know where they live now. Dan told me. I'm sure he didn't think much about it, and why would he? I'm no stalker or creeper. But knowing where she lives does give me an idea. Quinn's gone for a week, and Tayler's alone in a new place. That's probably a little unnerving. I need to make sure she's okay. It's what friends do, right?

WHEN THE DOOR OPENS, I smile at the sight of her. She looks disheveled. And a little dirty. And a lot tense. Not only that, her arms are crossed and her hip is jutting out to the side. Defensive stance. I look behind her at four or five stacks of boxes. Moving into a new place is hard work. Looking back down at her, I say, "Babe."

One word. It seems to relax her. Her once tense face softens a bit. "Luke."

"Can I come in?" I ask, holding up a box of Jeff's pizza in one hand and a six-pack of beer in the other. "I came to feed you." And to apologize, but I'll get to that in a bit.

Her arms drop to her side and she steps back. "Sure. I could eat."

Stepping into her new apartment, I smile. "This is cool." It has character, high ceilings covered in tin, and it's big and open. "How'd you score this place?" There had to be a wait list.

"It was all Quinn. She charmed the hell out of the owner and his dog."

"Yeah?" I could see that. Quinn is a sweet girl.

I watch Tayler move into her kitchen. Up on her tiptoes, she reaches into a cupboard to retrieve two plates. "She also didn't put up with any bullshit from the man. I wish I'd recorded it for posterity."

I follow her into the space and set the pizza on the counter. Opening up the fridge, I pull two bottles from the pack and put the rest in to stay cool. "She's somethin'."

"She is." Tayler giggles as she sets the plates down. "Fierce is the first word to come to mind to describe her now, because that's nothing like the Quinn from high school."

My thoughts turn to Tayler in high school. I bet she was a stunner even then. Not that it was that long ago, but still. She's a woman now, but I bet even as a girl, she was spectacular. Staring at her I realize how much I've missed her. *A lot.*

As Tayler turns around again to get something else, I move in closer. By the time she's turned back my way, she bumps into me. Taking advantage of that, I wrap my arms around her and pull her close. With one hand on her back and the other on her face, I whisper, "I'm sorry."

"Oh." Tayler's voice is soft and a little husky. Her head moves up slowly. When our eyes meet, she whispers, "Me too."

God, I want to kiss her. *So bad.* I can't, though, so I lean down slowly. It's then I hear her breath hitch. She's not moving either. Does she want me to kiss her? She has to know what it'd mean. Temporary.

I do the right fucking thing and kiss her forehead. You know, like a guy kisses his sister. I can feel the disappointment radiate off her in waves. She's out of my arms in less than a second and reaching into the pizza box in a second more.

She wanted me to kiss her. Hell, I wanted to. But I couldn't pull the trigger, and I know, without a doubt, that it was a mistake. There's no goin' back from that. I've lost her, at least the part of her that would have been in my bed. I'm sure *friend* Tayler is still there, but the other? Gone.

Yep. I'm fucked from that forehead kiss. Totally and completely fucked.

CHAPTER THIRTEEN

Tayler

"And then he kissed my forehead." I'm on an early morning walk with the ladies from Beedle. Well, everyone but Susanna. Apparently, she has a guy over, so it's only Patsy, Robbi, Kat, and Lindsay. I must have said something funny because all four of them are laughing hysterically.

When they finally calm down, Robbi's the first to speak. "He kissed your forehead? Like a priest?"

The cackling starts right back up. This time, I join them. It can't be helped.

"Father Luke," Patsy adds between breaths.

"Forgive me, Father, for I have sinned." Kat joins in the fray.

"Or not," Robbi deadpans. "It sounds like you'd like to sin with the sexy Luke Green."

That stops my laughter. Not anyone else's. Even though we're walking at a fast clip, I'm still able to turn a little and look at Robbi. "I'd love to sin. I just can't figure how to do it without feeling really shitty about myself afterward."

"Why the fuck would you feel shitty?" Robbi practically scoffs those words. "Having sex out of wedlock isn't a sin."

"I know." Eye roll. "I lived with Dylan. That's not it."

"Then what's your *real* issue with Luke Green?" Patsy's voice is much less abrasive than Robbi's. Don't get me wrong, I love Robbi's way of approaching things. You never have to wonder how she feels.

I have to think about her question, though, because something about the way she asked gives me pause. "I don't have an issue with him." On the contrary. "Um." My walk has slowed. Then I stop completely.

"What?" Kat has moved to stand beside me.

God, Quinn would shit a brick if she were here. The second she gets wind of my reason, she won't let me forget it. How many years did I give her crap about all the guys she used to love from afar and now I'm basically doing the same? "Short answer?" I look at the girls. "I think it's because he's my dream man." I thought about him in that way even when I was with Dylan. As shitty as that sounds, it's true. And nothing Luke has done so far, not even his bad attitude, has changed that. In fact, the more I know about Luke Green, the more I believe he's more than my dream man. He's my person.

"Ah." I'm not sure which one of them says that.

Surprisingly, it's Robbi who has the best response. "And you don't just fuck your dream man."

I shake my head. "No. You don't." You marry him.

"Babe."

I shake my head when I see the man standing in my doorway for the third night in a row. Quinn will be back the day after tomorrow, so I figure these little visits will stop then. In the meantime, I'm going to enjoy them. "What'd you bring tonight?"

He holds up a brown paper bag. "Burgers, fries, and some fried pickles for you. And I promise, no stacked meat."

"Yum." I walk to my kitchen knowing he'll be right behind me with the food. I reach for clean plates from my cupboard, but as I'm stretching out, I freeze when I feel his body right behind mine.

"I got 'em," he says in his deep voice—so deep I feel it rumbling on my back. I like it. Way too much.

I remain still until he's got the plates and he's moved back. Clearing my throat, I ask, "Something to drink?"

He doesn't answer, just opens my fridge and grabs the last two beers from the six-pack he brought the first night.

We move to the couch like we have the other nights. It's starting to feel really comfortable. Correction: comfortable isn't the right word because I'm not comfortable due to all the tension I feel between us, but I've grown accustomed to him being here. "What do you feel like watching?" I ask right before I eat my first fried pickle. *Yum.*

"Anything."

"Well"—I pick up the remote—"since cable is included in our rent, I'll choose something you may like." I flip channels until I find HGTV. "*Flip or Flop* is on."

"Never seen it." I watch him take a huge bite of his burger. I can't help noticing he's eating a single cheeseburger too. I snicker. "You know, *you* can eat stacked meat."

"Nah. I'd rather eat three burgers. More bread." He takes another giant bite, and I want to growl because guys suck. They can eat anything and never gain a pound. So not fair.

"We could watch a movie, but you probably need to get back to the bar." I look up at him, expecting him to agree, but he doesn't.

"I'm off now. Got Chris to take over."

"Oh." I'm happily surprised. "Want to watch something?"

Pulling another burger from the sack, he nods. "Sure. You pick."

Crap. That's not an easy task. I wouldn't want to choose the wrong movie. On the other hand, I don't want to sit through something I won't enjoy. Picking up the remote, I click on the OnDemand button and choose one of the movie channels. We have several—thank you, Vic. Scrolling through the options, I hesitate to point out something when he says, "You ever see *The Big Lebowski?*

I shake my head.

"It's a classic."

I highly doubt that, but when I find the movie, I read the description. I do love Jeff Bridges. Shrugging, I hit Play. Might as well check it out. "If I don't like it, can I change it?"

Luke chuckles. "Your house, your rules."

I like the sound of that.

As the movie rolls, I understand why he likes it. It's dark, quirky humor. Having finished my food, I set my plate on the table and scoot closer to him. That's when he slides his arm behind me and begins to run his long fingers through my ponytail.

OMG. I love having my hair played with.

In a matter of minutes, my eyes are half closed, but I'm still listening to the movie. His fingers are so gentle, it relaxes me.

"You like that?" His voice is deep and so damn sexy.

"Love it."

"Take your hair thing out."

Without hesitation, I reach back and pull out the hair tie, then sigh as he runs his fingers through my now loose hair. "Oh my God." I moan.

His hand stops suddenly. I'm about to voice my protest when I'm pushed onto my back and Luke Green is above me. "You can't make fucking noises like that, babe."

I blink up at him and smile. I love him like this. Above me. "Why not? It felt good." Yeah, I'm poking the bear.

He stares down at me. Just stares. I stare right back.

The tension is building between us, and I want to be the one to break it. Or add to it. So I do something I probably shouldn't: I reach out and rest my hand on the back of his neck. As I pull him closer, I lift my head. When my lips are less than an inch from his, Luke growls, "You don't want this."

"Oh, I *want* this." *Bad.*

Without another word, Luke slams his mouth against mine and takes control. His lips are firm but not stiff. They're moving, sliding, suckling on mine. When I feel his tongue touch my lips, I open for him. This damn kiss is one for the record book. How can one kiss make my body come to life like never before? I'm practically shaking from head to toe. The hands he'd had on either side of my head, the ones that were holding him above me, are now beneath me, which means we're pressed together. One is behind my head, the other on my lower back. He's surrounding me. I work to get my legs untangled beneath him until they're around him, Luke's center against mine. I moan again. That's when he presses down and I feel him. He's hard.

"Fuck." Luke pulls back from me before I can finish my thought. "Jesus, Tayler...." We're now separated completely and getting more so because Luke's off the couch and stomping toward the kitchen. I push myself up and turn so I can see what he's doing. He's looking down with his hands on his hips. His breathing is labored, like mine is. "We can't do that."

"Why not?" I mean, seriously. *Why not?* Sure, we're friends, but I know we're more than that. It seems like it, anyway.

He finally looks at me. "You know why not."

"Because you only like booty calls?"

He laughs, but there's no humor in it. "You could say that." He takes in a lungful of air and steps closer to me. "This is never going to be a romance, honey. I know you want more than a fuck now and then."

I blush at his words. "I thought...."

"You thought we were turning into something." It wasn't a question. "That's my fault. I like spending time with you, but I see now that you were reading too much into it."

I'm still just looking at the guy. I know I'm blinking twice as much as usual, and that could be to stem the tide of tears that are just sitting there. Tears that I will not allow to fall in front of him.

"I'd better go." He starts toward the door but stops. Without looking back at me, he asks, "You want help cleaning up?"

I stare some more, but when his question hits me, I flinch. "No." I don't want fucking help cleaning up. "I don't need a thing from you, Luke. You run along now." I stand up so I can lock the door behind him. Keeping my head held high. Yes, my nose is in the air, but it's the way it has to be.

"Babe."

Holding up my hand, I focus on calmness. "Just so you know, I was a little confused about *us*." I point back and forth between us. How could I not be? "Sure, I knew where you stood and that there is no *us*. I'm fine with that. I crossed the line, pulling you in for a kiss, and I'm sorry for it." More than he'll ever know. "It won't happen again."

Luke's turn to flinch.

"But hear this." I'm now a foot from the man. "I'm done here. You need to step back. Don't 'stop over.' Don't bring me food like it's a goddamn date."

"Babe—"

I halt him with my hand again. "Stop using endearments like 'babe'"—I say the word in a stupid deep voice—"and 'honey.' I'm not your honey." Obviously. "Don't act like a boyfriend if you don't want to be one."

"We're friends."

Shaking my head, I walk to the door, turn the knob, and open it for him. "No. We're not friends."

His head jerks back at my words, and a tiny part of me feels guilty for it, but I meant it.

"Go home, Luke. Have a good life." *Without me.*

"You're serious?" He's got both hands on his hips now. "You're done with me?"

Now it's my turn to flinch. "I never had you to be 'done' with in the first place. You never let me in. I can't be done with someone who only let me see the surface. You never allowed me to be part of the friendship. This thing with us was always on your terms. A real friendship goes both ways."

A tear slides down my cheek, and I feel it because it's burning a line down my face.

"Yeah," he says, stepping over the threshold. "Whatever."

And then he's gone.

"Shit." More tears fall. "Shit, shit, shit."

I miss him already. So damn much.

CHAPTER FOURTEEN

Luke

Her words hit hard. I didn't know what to say just then, but now that I'm in my car and I've had a few minutes to think, it pisses me off.

Me: I let you in. Literally. I never invite people into my home. That wasn't enough for you, though. You always wanted more.

More than I could give.

I wait a few minutes for her to respond. She doesn't, so I start up my engine and drive home. My anger increasing with each passing block.

I hear the ding of my message app and choose to wait until I get home to look. I need to focus on the road. Once I'm in my driveway, I pick it up and read.

Forever Girl: I'm sorry.

I'm sorry? What the fuck does that mean? What's she sorry for?

Me: For what?

Forever Girl: For hoping.

Jesus.

∽

I FEEL LIKE SHIT. Like I've got the flu. Aches, pains, that kind of thing, which is weird because I don't get sick. I eat healthy, relatively, and work out almost every day. I make it a point to at least get a run in on my treadmill. So the fact that all I want to do is sleep is troublesome.

I do the right thing and take the night off. I need to hire a couple more people so I'm not always relying on Chris. He's got a full load of classes that aren't easy. But I know he needs the money so that's something, I guess.

Grabbing the pillow and blanket off my bed, I make myself comfortable on my couch. When I can't find a damn thing to watch, I grab the remote for the DVD player and power it up. *The Shining* starts up, and for a split second, I feel a pang of something in my chest.

Maybe I've got a chest cold coming on.

I opt not to watch the movie that is forever going to remind me of the night I slept next to Tayler all night long.

God, I feel like shit.

Screw a movie. I just need to have something on in the background so I can sleep, finally. I need noise around me to make my brain stop working—to stop worrying. About what? I'm not sure. Something is definitely off with me.

I find an NHL game. The soft sounds of skates swishing on ice is all I need. Lying back, I cover myself and reach for the water I poured earlier. About to sip from it, I hear my phone chime. "Damn it." I left it in my bedroom. "Maybe it's Tay—"

Shut up, Luke.

Jogging into my room, I grab my cell and check it on my way back to the couch. I feel my body grow tight when I see the name on the screen. *Shanna.*

Shanna: Hey, stud. Long time no see.

Long time no see? No shit. That's by design. I've no interest in seeing, speaking to, or even texting my ex-wife. So I ignore it. Until another chime sounds.

Shanna: I know you're home sick.

She's been to the bar. Fuck. I told her to stay away from Cy's.

Shanna: Do you need anything, sweetums?

Sweetums? She used to call me that whenever she wanted something, and that was all the damn time, so...

I ignore the text.

Shanna: If you don't respond, I'm just going to head over to your place.

How the fuck does she know where I live?

Me: I'm fine. Contagious. Don't come over.

Shanna: Liar.

Yeah, *I'm* the liar.

Shanna: We need to talk.

Me: No. We don't. We...

I don't get to finish that message because my phone rings.

Fucking Shanna.

"What?" Don't say it. I know I'm an asshole, but there's no love lost between me and my ex.

"Nice." She laughs, and it makes my skin crawl. It's her "tinkling" laugh, and it's fake as fuck.

"I asked you a question. What do you want?"

"Jeez, Luke." I hear her make that snorty/scoffy noise. "Fine. I'll cut to the chase. I need a favor."

A favor? I know all about her favors by now. She's never stopped wanting shit from me. "No."

"You don't even know what it is!" Shanna's voice just rose an octave. This is going to get worse. I know because I lived with her for a couple of years, and I saw every "Shanna" she had in her arsenal; believe me, there were a bunch.

"Then what is it?"

"God, can't we even take a moment to catch up? Don't you care what I've been doing? It's been nearly three years."

Not long enough. "Fine. What have you been up to?" I'm sure it relates to the favor anyway.

"I'm glad you asked." She giggles again.

I want to pound the OFF button on my phone down onto the table. This is going to be good. Or bad, rather.

"I've been taking classes."

Eye roll. Shocker. She's got to have about a million college credits by now.

"And I've discovered my true calling."

Sure she has. This is probably no different than the other "callings" I paid for in the past. "Uh-huh."

"I'm nearly done with my degree in massage therapy."

"Degree?"

"Well." She laughs. "My certification."

"Uh-huh." That should make about five or six "certifications" in various other fields.

"I can hear you. The way you just said 'Uh-huh' tells me you're dubious."

"Uh-huh." Dubious as fuck.

"I'm ignoring that because you're not going to be dubious anymore. You're going to be grateful because I've got a great opportunity for you."

Opportunity = she needs Luke's money. "No."

"God, asshole. Hear me out."

"No."

"Such a dick," she hisses. "You never, ever believed in me. How many times did you tell me I needed a profession? Something to occupy my time." It sounds like there may be some sobs coming soon. Remember what I told you? I've seen all the Shanna's. Here comes sad, pathetic Shanna. The one she uses when she wants to guilting me into shit. It's not gonna work. Not this time.

"Just spit it out." So I can say no one more time. Then I can sleep, maybe.

"I need an investor. I want to open my own message therapy business."

"No."

And there it is. It feels damn good.

"Jesus." Shanna's voice has reached an all-time high. "You are *such* an asshole."

Ignoring her insult, I give her some good advice, "Get a loan from a bank, Shanna. They love to invest in women's businesses these days."

Through sniffles, she replies, "I tried."

"Sorry, but my money is all tied up in *my* business." As well as this house, but she doesn't need to know about that.

"You could take out a loan against..."

"Shanna." I'm getting pissed now. "I will never—and I mean never—loan *you* money." I'd never get it back and forget about interest. "We settled up after the divorce. You got a shit-ton of *my* money." *All* of my money that was in savings. I had to pay her off because she wanted part ownership of Cy's. My baby—my bar. No way.

"But, you have *so* much money." Whining isn't going to get her anywhere.

"No, I really don't. Besides, that's none of your fucking concern anymore, Shanna." My breathing is getting labored. I literally hate this woman. She made my life a living hell after I asked her for a divorce. Before then, it wasn't a fuck-ton of fun either. "I'm hanging up. Have a good life, and leave me the fuck alone."

I hang up. It wasn't satisfying enough. I mean, pressing the red button instead of slamming down the receiver on a real phone? There's no comparison.

I flop back onto the couch and close my eyes. "A loan?" I laugh to myself but stop suddenly. My mind goes to Tayler. Seemingly Shanna's opposite, but I used to think Shanna was sweet like that. The minute I put a ring on her finger, though, everything changed. She wanted shit. A big new house, for one. Nothing like this place I ended up buying. She'd hate this house.

It makes me smile when I remember how much Tayler loved

the old Craftsman bungalow. I guess the two aren't so similar, and after that call, I'm even more confused about Tayler. She's nothing like Shanna. This I know for certain. But it changes nothing. Even if Tayler were the perfect woman for me—it still wouldn't make be believe I'm capable of a relationship. I'm not.

I place my palm over my heart and wince. "Must be a chest cold coming on." I relax into my couch and close my eyes. The sounds of hockey on the television in the background help relax me, and I fall asleep.

CHAPTER FIFTEEN

Tayler

"So how was it?" I ask Quinn on the car ride back to Ames. I picked her up at the airport after her week-long trip to London.

"Amazing. Perfect. He told me he loves me."

Holy shit.

I nearly put the car in the ditch from her pronouncement. "Shut the front door! Did you say it back?"

I'm holding my breath because this is huge. More than huge. My best friend, and the sweetest girl in the world, has been in love, or thought she was, with maybe five guys. Five guys who didn't know she existed, at least not in the romantic sense. And for that guy, Cooke Thompson, professional rugby sensation and hottest man in the world (not kidding), to tell her he loves her? Well, that's just... just....

"I did." She smiles. "I do love him."

I smirk. "What's not to love?"

And then the most magnificent thing happens. The thing I've wanted for my sweet friend to say forever. "He's not perfect."

I feel the car jerk to my left. Shit. I nearly put my car in the ditch. It's official. I'm going to kill us. To get the car back to rights, I slow it down, then pull off onto the next exit ramp. This conversation needs to happen in a stopped vehicle anyway. But first, I need to hug her.

Quinn laughs. "Did you miss me that much?"

I let her go. I've got to say this, "You haven't put Cooke on a pedestal. You said it yourself, he's not perfect."

"He's *not* perfect, but he's perfect for me."

"But every other guy you've ever lusted after was *perfect*. Nothing was ever wrong with them. Take Bryant." I snort because Bryant is a douchebag. "You thought he shit sunshine."

"Gross. I did not." Quinn's laughing. She knows it's true.

"Yes, you did. But this *hot British* guy... a professional athlete who's loaded—I assume. *That* guy isn't perfect?"

"No. He's sort of a slob, and he's super cranky in the morning, and—"

"See?" God, I'm excited. "This is fucking awesome." I breathe a sigh of relief. Something I've been holding in forever as it relates to Quinn. She always worried me with her crushes. But this one. This is real.

Putting the car back into Drive, I check the road making sure it's safe to go.

"You're crazy."

I look over at Quinn, "*You're* crazy. By the way, Vic has been asking about you every day. It's getting on my nerves, so you'd better stop in and tell him you're back."

"Aw, that's nice."

"He loves you for some reason. Hell, he can't even remember my name."

"He calls me spitfire."

"He called you Quinn to me."

"Maybe I'll take Mary for a walk or something."

"You should. Find out the story about her, would you? All Vic said was she was abused. I want to know if the fuckers who abused her were punished."

"I'll try."

"Good." At least that gives me something else to think about. Something other than Luke and the fact that I haven't heard a word from him for two nights. I suspect it's going to be much longer.

Changing the subject, I announce, "I think we should have a dinner party. You know, to christen the new place."

"Ooh, what a great idea." Quinn says excitedly. "We could invite the rugby guys and the Beedle Babes."

Quinn gets quiet suddenly.

"What?"

Turning to face me, I glance at her then back to the road. In that split second, I can tell she feels bad about something. "I'm so sorry I wasn't there to help unpack."

I shake my head and pat her leg with my right hand. "No worries, your stuff still needs to be unpacked." I snort. "As for the rest of it, Luke..." No. Not going there.

"Luke what? You can't leave me hangin', girl."

"Nothing." I press down on the accelerator so we can get home faster.

"Spill, biatch."

I laugh from surprise. "He stopped by a couple of times. He helped me unpack some things one of those times." The second night. He even came with a box cutter to speed up the process.

"Didn't you help him paint his room or something?"

"Yeah. That's true. He was just returning the favor."

"Well, we'll have to invite him to our little dinner party."

No. "I'll see if he can get away from work." I'm lying. I'm not asking him. No way.

"Cool. I'll tell the girls on our next walk." She pulls her phone out of her purse. "I need to check my messages."

I hear her say, "Aw," and from that alone, I know it's from Cooke. "He misses me."

"I bet he does."

And then it hits me. Quinn could leave. She could move to England and leave me behind.

Thinking of life without her makes me feel sick to my stomach. But I won't let it ruin our reunion or her happiness. She deserves it.

QUINN MUST'VE INVITED Luke to our dinner party because I sure as hell didn't. Honest to God, I'm shocked he showed up. What's his deal? He's been here for almost an hour and he hasn't said boo to me. It's weird because no matter where I go in my place, there he is. No worries. Dinner is almost ready, so as soon as that's done, he'll go back to work. It can't happen soon enough, because just having him here is making my heart hurt.

Doing my best to shutter my emotions, I focus on the pasta. Quinn and I decided to make spaghetti for our guests, mainly because it's cheap and it's easy to doctor up the sauce so it doesn't taste like crappy stuff from the can. As I taste test the bubbling red sauce, I feel someone at my back. I know who it is before a word comes out of the jerk's mouth. I know because one, I can smell him, and two, I just do.

"We need to talk." His voice is low, almost a whisper.

I don't bother with being quiet. "No. We really don't."

"Yeah we do."

"No, we don't." I'm getting angry, and now I can't move back because he's so stupidly close. Gah! This guy.

"I just need a minute of your time, babe."

I suck in air and close my eyes. Well, they're pinched shut, actually, because "babe"? Really? With gritted teeth, I'm able to say, "Stop calling me babe." *You frigging jerk.*

"Give me five minutes, Tayler."

I get the sense he wanted to finish that sentence with something like "you owe me," but he didn't. A good thing too.

"Fine." I tap the spoon hard against the pot and set it on the counter. Turning to Quinn, who has been doing her best to pretend nothing is going down with Luke and me, I chirp, "Back in a minute, Q."

"Yep," she says as she busily gets the garlic bread ready for the oven.

He follows me to my bedroom. Crossing over the threshold to my room, I wait for him to move into my personal sanctuary, then shut the door. I cross my arms in front of me and snap, "What?"

"Nice room."

He's looking at my bedroom?

When he opens up my closet door, I want to scream, but I don't. "Wow, great closet. I get why you like this place. The bathroom is nice too."

I'm not doing this. "What. Do. You. Want?"

Hell, I should just ask him why he's here. Why did he come to this dinner party?

Shutting the closet door, he takes two steps closer to me. "Look." Running his fingers through his hair—which is getting pretty long, actually—he sighs. "I'm sorry how things ended."

Ended?

I hate that word. I don't mean to, but my palm goes to that spot right over my heart; then I quickly remember myself and let it drop down to my side.

"There was nothing wrong with you kissing me. It just can't happen again."

I'm blinking. That's it. I'm not even sure I'm breathing, but I must be. "What are you saying?"

He shakes his head. "Just that. You shouldn't feel bad that you kissed me."

What a jerk. "I don't."

"Sure you do. You've got guilt written all over you. Don't feel bad about it. It was nothing."

The pain in my chest is now radiating out. Am I having a

heart attack? No. It's not that kind of pain. This kind is more embarrassment.

It was nothing?

I certainly didn't think it was nothing.

"I'll still be your friend."

I need to get my shit together. This guy is talking way too much. "Well, gee, Luke." I scoff because I'm having a hard time processing all of this *fucking bullshit.* "While I appreciate you granting me the *privilege* of being your friend"—I reach for the doorknob—"I decline." I pull on the door, but it won't budge. I look down and see Luke's giant foot is blocking it from moving.

"Tayler...."

I shake my head. "No." Looking up at him, I feel a sense of loss I can't really explain. "I know how friendship works, Luke. And you aren't good at it." I jab a finger at his hard chest. "It's all Luke all the time. Everything is on your terms, and that's not how friendship works."

Luke rolls his eyes, and I'd laugh if I weren't pissed and hurting. "I know how it works too, and friends don't kiss friends."

"See?" I quip. "That's the difference. I have feelings for you. The 'more than friends' kind of feelings." Shit. I shouldn't have admitted that, but it's out there now. "That makes the friend-zone thing difficult."

"I have feelings for you too, Tayler. Only mine are the 'fuck you once so I can forget about you' kind of feelings."

I jerk my head back in shock. I mean, that hurt. I feel the familiar burn of tears behind my eyes, but I won't let him see. "Well, then." I place my hand on his chest and push, hoping he gets the hint and moves away from the door. But he doesn't. "Move," I snap. "Let me out. I have real friends in the other room. People who were actually invited—"

"I was invited."

Not by me. "Please. Move."

"Tayler, come on."

I swallow hard because my throat feels all closed up. I'm ashamed to say what I do next, but it always worked with Dylan. Want a guy to leave you alone? Cry. So, that's what I do. Those tears that were sitting below the surface are now pouring from my eyes. It works too. Luke backs up enough for me to yank the door open. Then he wraps his arm around me from behind, hauling me back into my bedroom. The door slams shut and I'm off the ground.

"Luke." It's watery sounding but audible. "Put me down."

"No," he says, walking toward my bed.

"Yes. Dinner's almost ready."

"It'll wait." He says it as he spins around so he can sit on my mattress.

Luke's still got his arms around me, but I'm no longer off the ground. My feet are planted between his legs. Thankfully, I'm facing away from him. I haven't stopped crying, but it's slowed some.

"Tayler." His voice is soft. "I know that was hard for you to hear, but it's the truth."

God, every time I think he's going to say something nice, he fucking doesn't.

"There will never be anything romantic between us."

I just nod because if I speak, it's going to be a sort of blubbering.

"Yeah?"

I nod again.

"Can you look at me?"

I need to get the hell out of this room, and the only way to achieve that is to just agree with the asshole. His arms are still around me, but they've loosened, so I slowly rotate in his arms. His hand moves closer to my face like he wants to wipe away the tears, but I beat him to it. "I'm good." Not really. Not at all, actually.

"Can we still be friends?"

Is he for real?

"Sure." I nod. "Absolutely."

Lies. All lies.

"Good."

I feel him tugging me closer, which causes me to stiffen up—like a corpse. "What are you doing?"

"Was gonna kiss your forehead."

"No thanks." I wiggle until he finally releases me. "I need to go check my face in the bathroom and finish dinner."

Luke sighs, sounding resigned. "Sure. Good."

Good? God, I'm exhausted. Literally. I could sleep for days after all of this emotional bullshit with Luke Green.

"Good." I quickly open my door and make a beeline for my bathroom. Inside, I stand stock-still, using the moment to gather myself. I've got no time to think about all of his words. It'll have to wait until later, when I'm alone.

CHAPTER SIXTEEN

Luke

"Come on, Quinn. Hurry the hell up." I'm yelling at her from the top of the stairs. She's gone down to retrieve a couple cases of bottled beer, and it's taking her twice as long as usual. "Quinn?"

"What?" Her voice startles me, probably due to the fact that it's coming from behind me.

Turning, I snap, "I told you to get—"

"I did." Quinn rolls her eyes. "You were chatting up that blonde, so you didn't see me."

"I wasn't chatting up the blonde." I definitely was. She offered to meet up later, but I haven't committed to that yet. I think I should, though. It'll get my mind off the fact that Tayler Sorenson is no longer a fixture in my life.

I laugh and it sounds a little dry. Fixture? Ha! That'd mean she's a fixed part of my life, and there's no truth to that whatsoever. As a matter of fact, I haven't seen or heard from her for weeks, not since the dinner party. I can't say I blame her. When I went back over the bullshit that spewed from my mouth—*"I have feelings for you too, Tayler. Only mine are the 'fuck you once so I can forget about you' kind of feelings."*—well, let's just say I wouldn't talk to me either.

Truth be told, I miss her. A lot. No way am I admitting that to anyone else, though. It's for the best.

"So." Quinn tosses a bar towel over her shoulder, her arms are crossed in front of her, and she's tapping the toe of her worn-out black Converse tennis shoes on my concrete floor.

"Yeah?" I don't think I'm going to like this.

"When are you gonna pull your head out of your ass?"

"Excuse me?" The insubordinate little—

"About Tayler."

I lower my voice because it's busy tonight. "What about Tayler?"

Quinn tilts her head and narrows her eyes. "You like her."

"What's not to like?" I shrug like an asshole. "I'm not looking for a wife, Quinn."

Her crinkled nose tells me more than words. "She doesn't want to marry *you*."

Wow, that kind of wounded me a little. "No?" I'm really asking. Did she mean that?

"No way." Quinn shakes her head back and forth, over and over. "You'd drive her crazy with all your aloofness."

"Aloofness." I'm just trying the word out to see if it fits. It does.

"Yeah. Some would say cold, but I'd have to disagree."

"Cold."

"It's not cold. You're just a very high-maintenance man."

That one makes me chuckle. "I'm not fucking high maintenance." When she massages her temples, I stare for a second. "I'm not."

"Sure." She pats my arm. "That's what all high-maintenance people say." Turning, she pauses. Looking at me over her shoulder, Quinn adds, "Oh, and reminder. Cooke's going to be here the day after tomorrow to start rehab, so you'll need to find someone to cover for me during my hiatus."

Hiatus? That's what she's calling it? Now who's fucking high maintenance? "You're gonna leave me short-handed. Again." I haven't even started looking for someone else, which means my hours here are going to increase, which also means that my house projects will be put on hold.

Quinn scratches her cheek. "Yeah. Sorry about that." There's a pause and then, "I know someone who needs a job, though."

No.

"At least she could work here over the holiday break."

Oh, here we go. "No."

"Why not? She's got bartending experience. She used to work at the country club back home." Quinn looks tentative, but it doesn't stop her. "Oh, and she has no idea I brought that up, so we could pretend it was your idea."

Now that makes no sense. Why would Tayler want to be anywhere near me?

"She needs the money, though."

She does? "Is she okay?"

Quinn shrugs. "Mostly. School's stressing her out. Money is stressing her out, and that jerk Dylan wants her back. He's getting sort of creepy about it." She stops talking for a second. "Shit. Don't tell her I told you all of that. She'll kill me."

I ignore that first bit, needing to know more about her ex-asshole. What the fuck does that mean? "What's Dylan doing?"

She shakes her head quickly. "I promised I wouldn't tell you, so forget I mentioned it."

The hell? That's not gonna work. "Is she in danger?"

"Oh." Quinn looks up like she's giving my question some thought. "Probably not." She waits a beat. "Maybe?"

Fuck.

And then it hits me. I shake my finger at her. "Oh, I know what you're doing."

She turns back, looking coy. "I'm not doing a thing."

"Are you trying to worry me so I'll go over and check on her?" Because it's working.

I watch Quinn's face turn from puzzled to smiling wide. "Wow. I'm flattered you think I could be that devious." She taps her chin with her finger. "I wonder if Cooke thinks I'm that sneaky." Pulling her phone from her back pocket, she begins to text.

"No fucking cell phones!"

"Oh." She titters nervously. "Oops." Sliding it into her back pocket, I watch her walk away.

"Bus the damn tables," I yell loud enough for everyone to hear. *This place is a mess.*

She lifts her hand and waves. I half expect to see her middle finger, but I don't. Instead, she begins to bus the table in front of her.

Good girl.

QUINN'S WORDS keep tumbling around in my head. Tayler is broke, she's stressed, and most importantly, what's her ex doing? I wish I knew.

I left the bar soon after our conversation because the headache I've been fighting off is back. I touch my forehead; positive the fever is back too. I need to go to the doctor, but why when over-the-counter medicine seems to help most of the symptoms? Not the pain in my upper torso, though. For *that*, I probably do need to see the doc. Still, it's not a constant pain—it comes and goes.

Changing out of my jeans, I throw on some sweats in preparation of sitting on my couch for the rest of the night. I touch my head again and decide I do feel a little feverish. Retrieving some aspirin from my bathroom medicine cabinet, I also find a lone beer in my fridge. Sure, I know it's not a great idea to mix meds with beer, but who gives a fuck?

Not me.

Back on the couch, I look around my living space. Tayler was going to tell me what color I should paint this room. I wonder what she chose. I bet it was the perfect color. Most likely something true to the Craftsman style of the house. I bet she'd have ideas for the kitchen too. It'd make sense since she wants to design interiors.

"I should ask her."

My head chooses that second to pound. Lying down, I grab the lone pillow I've got on my sofa. Placing my hand on my head again, I moan. Yeah, that's what I said, I moan. I can't help it. I feel like shit.

CHAPTER SEVENTEEN

Luke

I couldn't stop picturing Tayler in trouble. Hell, I had dreams about it. I tossed and turned all night long. Sure, part of that was because I felt terrible, but most of it was concern for Tayler.

I woke up this morning shaky, still on my sofa, with the same headache I fell asleep with. Deciding to work through it, I got up and made coffee. As soon as that brewed, I took it back to the couch with me. While I sipped, I remembered the dreams. The most vivid one was me searching in the dark for her. I kept hearing her voice. She sounded scared, which made my heart race, but I kept looking for her. When she screamed, I swear part of me wanted to kill whoever was hurting her.

Shit. *Was it me?*

It could have been. Dreams are weird like that. Ironic.

Resting my head in my hands, it hits me. I know what I need to do, and she's not gonna like it. Not one bit.

I SHOULDN'T BE HERE. Tayler's probably going to kick my ass, and it's all Quinn's fault.

Raising my hand to knock on her door, I pause and lean in closer to listen. It's early, plus it's Saturday, so she should be home. When I hear nothing, I knock again. Still nothing. Pulling out the phone from my back pocket, I text Quinn.

Me: I'm at your door. Come let me in.

I wait two or three minutes and knock again. That's when I hear a voice. Quinn. She pulls the door open, and I want to laugh. She looks like she's been in a wind tunnel, only not in a good way. "Hey."

"What on God's green earth are you doing here at six in the morning? On. A. Saturday? I worked until close last night, and I'm pooped."

"I need to see Tayler."

With one brow arched, Quinn's mouth begins to open like she's about to say something, most likely something snarky, but she stops when Tayler steps into the living room. The second I catch a glimpse of her, something sort of miraculous happens. My headache? Gone.

"Tayler." My voice catches like I haven't spoken for weeks.

"Luke?" Tayler's voice is husky and sleepy but sweet at the same time. "What are you doing here?" Shit. She sounds sad.

I step through the doorway past a shockingly silent Quinn. "I need to talk to you."

"You do?"

I do. You know what else? The closer I get to her, the better I feel. The pressure in my chest is lessening. "I do."

"Why?"

"I'm going back to bed." I forgot Quinn was even there, but now that she's spoken, I'm glad she's leaving us alone.

I look down at Tayler. I'm just going to do it. I'm going to say it. I have to. "I've missed you." Plus, I'm worried about her too, but I'll get into that later.

Tayler's beautiful face flushes a gorgeous shade of pink, but that doesn't stop her from saying the four best words I've ever heard. "I've missed you too."

Not sure what to do next, I hold up the white paper sack in my hand. "Brought you donuts."

"Oh?" Then the most beautiful thing happens. She laughs, and I swear to you, my previous body aches disappear. It's like she's the best medicine I've ever taken.

In case you're wondering, no, it's not lost on me that my previous ills were probably brought on by the fact that I think I need this woman. My body was telling me so, and it's rarely wrong about these things. My head, on the other hand? It's usually way off. In this case, though, my brain agrees. I just don't know what it means. Do I miss my friend, or is there more to this?

"It's a bit early for me to eat but let me make some coffee. I'll have one with a cup-a-joe." She giggles again as she makes her way into her kitchen.

I need to keep going. It seems like the more I say—*confess*—the better I feel, so why stop now? "I'm sorry about what I said to you at the dinner party. It was callous and mean. I just—"

Luckily, she stops me from spewing too much by holding up her pretty hand, "Me too, Luke. I swear—" She chuckles. "—you bring out the worst in me."

And you bring out the best in me.

I don't say it because I need to save something for when I fuck up again. And I *will* fuck up again.

"Have a seat."

I move to her couch and sit. I've still got the donuts, so I open the bag as she appears with two small plates and two cups of coffee, handing me my cup.

"Oh, I forgot to ask, how do you take your coffee?"

"Black." I'm about to joke about it being black like my heart, but I'm not going to ruin this with a stupid joke. One that she may take seriously.

"Ick." She scrunches up her nose. It's adorable. "I've got

Snickers-flavored coffee creamer if you want something really good."

"Ick," I say with my own scrunched-up nose. "I like it like this."

"Whatever." She lifts the white bag from the table and peeks inside. "Interesting selection." I watch as she reaches in. I'm holding my breath to see what she picks. I intentionally chose four different kinds of donuts since I wasn't sure what she'd prefer. What comes out of the bag surprises me.

"Jelly-filled?" Not only that, it's covered in powdered sugar. That means it's messy.

"Mm. Love me some jelly-filled." Her mouth opens wide, and as she bites, the groan I've got ready to release makes me freeze. I can't make sexy noises. Not right now, anyway.

I watch as the white powder floats down onto her chest. When I look up, I smile because half of her face is covered in white sugar. Damn, I'd like to lick that off of everything. For a split second I picture her naked, covered entirely in soft, white powdered sugar. I could lick.... I shake my head. I need to stop those thoughts. Getting a hard-on right now isn't the best idea.

"I'll, uh—" I'm mesmerized by the sight of her eating. "—remember that." To distract me, I grab the bag and reach in. I don't care what I get; I'll eat any of them. What I retrieve is a glazed cinnamon roll. Biting into it, I moan and nod at the same time. "Good."

Using the side of her hand, she wipes at her mouth. I should tell her she missed a glob of jelly, but I don't want to.

Again, I wonder what it'd be like to lick all that off.

Stop! Jesus, get it under control, Luke.

My dirty thoughts are interrupted by a knock at the door. The two of us look at each other. Then something flickers across her face. Fear? Annoyance?

No, it's fear. I swear it is.

"You want me to get it?"

She shakes her head quickly, back and forth. "No." When she stands, I notice her pajamas for the first time. She's got on an oversized Cy's Roost tee and a pair of tiny shorts that peek out from the bottom of the shirt. I love the look, personally, but... "Maybe you should change before you answer the door?"

She looks down at herself, then at me. The expression says it all. "I'm fine."

"I know. I just...." Shit. I need to shut up. Things are going well. I feel like my old self again.

Standing, I decide to walk with her to the door. She's up on her tiptoes, looking through the peephole. Glancing back at me, she whispers, "Dylan." as she opens the door. "Dylan. What are you doing here? It's early."

"Babe."

Babe?

He's dressed in a wrinkled tee and jeans. The clothes look like he slept in them. "I needed to see you."

I step behind her and place my hand on her shoulder. The asshole finally sees me. "Can I help you?" My voice sounds deep and ominous—by design.

He blinks repeatedly. "Who the...? Oh, Luke." He smiles. "Man, how are ya?"

"What do you want, Dylan?" Tayler asks again.

He looks at her and gives her a lopsided smile. "What's *he* doing here?"

I wait for her to speak, but she's silent. And stiff. As a board. So, I do something I probably shouldn't. "I'm with Tayler."

The silence is deafening. It's douchebag who breaks the quiet, though. Dylan glares at her and laughs. "What?"

Tayler's still silent, so I keep going. "For a while, man." I nod. "We wanted to keep it on the down-low 'til we knew for sure."

"Knew what?" Dylan's still glaring at Tayler, and it's pissing me the fuck off.

I've had it with his bullshit. Cutting to the chase, I just say, "She's mine." It comes out as more of a growl, but it's effective.

"Tayler." Dylan sounds a little snippy. Again, I don't like it. "Can we please speak in *private?*"

"No," I answer for her. Might as well keep going. "If you've got something to say in front of my woman, you say it to both of us."

"Dude. She was my girlfriend for four years. I should be able to—"

"You cheated on her. You lost any rights to do anything."

"Jesus." The fucker runs his fingers through his hair. "I love her."

"Ha!" Tayler finally speaks. "That's a joke."

"The fuck! I did—I do love you." Dylan is pacing back and forth in front of the door now.

I take one step closer to him, moving Tayler to the side. "Time to go home, man."

He stops pacing suddenly. His demeanor turns from agitated to cool and calm again. He chuckles, but it sounds high-pitched and creepy clown-like. Raising one hand, he shakes his head. "Sorry, man. You're right. I overstepped. I'll just take off."

"Good idea," I mutter.

The two of us watch him turn, walk quickly down the short hallway, and descend the stairs. As soon as he's out of sight, I shut the door, lock it, and turn to face her. "That shit is no joke."

Waving my words away like they mean nothing, she says, "He's harmless."

I step closer and place my hands on her upper arms. "Bullshit, babe. Quinn told me—"

"Shit."

The sound surprises us. We both turn to see Quinn walking into the kitchen. "I specifically told you not to tell her, asswipe."

I scoff. "After what I just saw at the door, you should have told me sooner."

Quinn shakes her head. "Tay wouldn't let me."

"I still didn't want you to say anything," Tayler snaps. "Jesus, what happened to best friends keeping a frigging secret? Huh?"

"Babe." I lean down so she's looking into my eyes. "When the situation turns dangerous, you do what you need to do to make sure your friends are safe."

"Dylan is not dangerous."

"What about the letters?" Quinn butts in.

"Quinn!" Tayler shouts. "Shut the hell up!"

I narrow my eyes. "What letters?"

Tayler ignores my question and stomps over to the table. Picking up the donuts, she rolls the bag shut and marches back to me. "Thanks for the donuts. You can go now."

I don't take the bag. Instead, I look over at Quinn, "Quinn, you need to call that cop friend of yours."

"No!" Tayler shouts.

"Yes. And show me the letters."

Tayler's voice is a screech level as she practically screams, "No!"

"Tell me what happened here this morning."

The three of us are sitting in Quinn and Tayler's living room telling Ames cop, Gage Golden, about Dylan's visit. He's been taking notes like crazy, so at least he's doing his due diligence even though it's obvious he's not on the clock. He's got on jeans, sneaks, and a Led Zeppelin t-shirt instead of his black cop clothes. No doubt he's here because of Quinn. It's obvious he considers her a friend. I know he was a big help to her when the shit went down with that crazy chick, Kara. And since then, I've seen him at Cy's a couple of times, usually alone. So, yeah, I'm glad *she's* got an ally on the police force because me and cops haven't always seen eye to eye. That was years ago, though. Now I'm an upstanding member of the community.

Ha! That's a joke.

Well, technically I am. I'd just never categorize myself as "upstanding." Take the shit this morning, for example. I wish it'd just been Dylan and me. Then I'd have made sure he knew never to 'stop by' Tayler's place again.

"Luke?"

"Oh, right. Sorry, man." I tell the story from my point of view, starting from my arrival at Tayler's place to Dylan's knock on the door. I attempt to remember everything that was said between the two of us. What I didn't get right, Tayler corrected me. The woman remembered everything.

So far, neither woman has mentioned the letters, and they sure as shit haven't shown them to me. "He's written some letters, but they won't let me see them."

Golden's brow arches. "Letters?"

"They're nothing," Tayler says defensively.

Quinn interjects, "Well, I wouldn't say they were nothing, hon."

"Quinn! Whose side are you on?"

"Yours. That's why I think you should at least show Gage. He's probably seen this kind of thing before. Let him decide if it's normal or not."

"Fine." Growling, Tayler stands and marches into the kitchen. Yanking open one of her kitchen drawers, she pulls out a plastic silverware holder and sets it on the counter. Next, she retrieves several pieces of paper. Back at the couch, she sets them on the table in front of Gage.

We watch as he slides on rubber gloves.

Tayler snaps, "They're in chronological order."

Quinn snorts. "'Course they are."

Standing, I move behind Gage so I can look down at the first letter. He doesn't protest, so I read:

. . .

Tayler,

I love you. I always will. Give me another chance. I screwed up. Nobody can hold a candle to you.

Love, Dylan

"That one doesn't seem so out of the ordinary." Gage sets it down and picks up a second letter.

Red,

I miss you so much. I saw you at HyVee yesterday. You were buying chicken and twice-baked potatoes. You know those are my favorites. Are you cooking me dinner? Just call. I'll be there.

Love, Dylan

I look over at Tayler who's staring down at the floor. She has to know this isn't normal.

A third letter reads:

Tayler,

You were wearing those jeans today that make your ass look so damn good. Are you wearing those for me? Can you feel me nearby, watching you? I don't like the way you're flirting with that kid from your psych class. Is there something going on with you two?

Dylan.

Well, that one was fucking creepy. But the more we read, the more surreal they get.

· · ·

TAYLER,

My woman. My future wife. I can't take it any longer. You need to know where I stand. I can't believe what a fool I was to think anyone else could compare to you. But listen to me clearly. I've learned my lesson. I even told my mom that I'll do whatever it takes to make you see that we belong together forever. Anything.

No worries, sweet Tayler. I'll be patient because no matter what, I know we'll always be together.

Yours, Dylan.

THE LAST SENTENCE is the one that makes my skin crawl. I can't believe he didn't follow it up with "If I can't have you, nobody will," because that's the kind of stalker bullshit this guy was spewing.

"Tayler, you should consider getting a protective order against Dylan. Each letter seems to get progressively more obsessive. Have you noticed him following you?"

"Following me?" She shakes her head. "Not really. I saw him every once in a while, on campus, but he's never approached me. I mean, he's taking classes too." Her voice is shaky. It's obvious this is getting to her. Not only that, her skin is ghostly pale.

Moving around the circle, I step behind her and place one hand on her shoulder, shifting close enough for her to feel my presence.

"It's apparent from his statements that he's been watching you on campus, at the store, and possibly other places."

I'm nodding as Gage speaks, but Tayler's shaking her head.

"Tayler," Gage scoots so he's on the edge of his seat. "This is serious. It's escalating. A protective over is the way to go."

"No. Our parents are friends. They wouldn't understand. It would make things awkward for them."

Fuck awkward.

My mouth is agape. Yep, I'm slack-jawed. "Honey." I squeeze her shoulder. "The guy is unstable...."

"Girl, you need a protective order," Quinn chimes in. "At least that will give Dylan the warning he needs to know he's crossed a line."

Tayler sighs as her shoulders slump. I can feel how defeated she is through my fingers. "Okay." Tayler sighs. "I'll call home."

"Okay?" I bend down so I can see her face. "You're going to get the protective order?" Please say yes.

"As soon as I talk to my folks. It's probably time, though." Tayler turns to Quinn and points a finger at her. "And you don't have any room to talk. You didn't want one on Kara the psycho."

"That was different."

"How?" Gage asks.

"She's a girl."

I release a short laugh. "Women are just as dangerous as men, Quinn. Don't be stupid."

"I'm not stupid." She gives me a thumbs-down. "You suck, Luke." Looking back at Gage, she adds, "She was a *small* girl."

Gage shakes that one off too. "She can drive a car. Look what she did to your scooter."

Quinn nods. "True dat."

Addressing Quinn, he adds softly, "I was going to call you today to let you know... it appears she's planning on moving back into her apartment."

My head is pinging back and forth between Quinn and Gage.

"To Ames?" Quinn's voice squeaks, "Her father promised."

"He said he'd 'try.' I asked the landlord to let me know what they did with her place. I was hoping they'd moved her out, but I got a message from them last night telling me that she's renewing her lease. She's moving back."

"When?"

"I don't have a date yet, but the second I get one, I'll let you know."

"That bitch," Tayler spits. "She'd better hope she never crosses my path. I'll fucking kill her."

"Now, now, Cujo." Quinn pats Tayler's hand. "One psycho at a time, babe. Let's deal with Dylan first."

"You both need to stay vigilant." Gage's warning sounds more ominous than I care for.

"I'm not gonna let anything happen to either one of them." I point my thumb at Quinn. "And her man will be here tomorrow."

Gage looks over at Quinn and asks softly. "Is that right?"

"Yep," she says with a bright smile.

I hope that guy doesn't break her heart. I'll kick his ass. It'll be easy since he's injured.

Needing to prove Tayler will be protected, I add, "I'm with Tayler, so I'll be sure she's safe." You know what? Now that I've said it aloud, I don't mind the sound of it.

I'm with Tayler.

No, I don't mind the sound of that at all.

CHAPTER EIGHTEEN

Tayler

"*I'm with Tayler....*"

My gaze is fixed on the man who just uttered those words. I can't believe he actually said them. *Out loud.* I mean, if you'd asked me last night if I'd ever see Luke Green again, I'd have said no. And now he's *with me*?

"Um." I hold up one finger. "Let's not put the cart before the horse, guys." I want to roll my eyes so badly, but I can't because this shit is serious. "Let me call home. Then, I'll get the protective order in place and go from there."

"But—"

Luke is going to contradict me? I was helping him out here.

"No." I shake him off. "We're getting off track. We're only guessing what Dylan was up to. I get that I need to make sure he stays away from me." *Big-time.* That last letter scared the bejesus out of me.

"More than stay away from you." Luke looks angry with brows furrowed and his lips drawn thin.

God, I want to get him alone so I can ask him why he really came over here. Was it because Quinn blabbed her stupid big mouth about Dylan, or did he really miss me? My guess is it was the former.

"I agree." Gage has slipped his small notebook into his back pocket. "We can get that process started today. You can meet me at the station this afternoon."

"I'll call my parents," I reply. "Quinn and I will come down to the station after that."

"I'm your man. *I'll* take you," Luke growls.

The eyeroll inside my head is aching to get out, but I hold it in. My goodness, when did he turn into this alpha-hole? "Dylan's gone. You can knock off the 'I'm your man' bullshit." I mean, seriously. "Quinn and I have plans today." Or we did. "She and I can handle going to the police station on our own."

Luke's glaring at me. "Can I speak to you for a second? In your bedroom."

"Fine." I turn and stomp out of the living room and into my bedroom. The second I step over the threshold; I turn and place my hands on my hips. I'm about to let him have it when large hands wrap around me and slide right below my ass cheeks. I feel myself being lifted, so I quickly grab at the only thing I can—Luke's shoulders. He's moving me back at a fast clip, and when I feel myself falling backward, I squeak. The soft landing lets me know I'm on my bed, and Luke is right there with me. He's so close, he's basically on top of me.

"Babe."

My eyes meet his. His turn from angry to soft. Mine? Not soft. I snap, "What?"

He says nothing, giving me his stupid smirk. "I need you to understand."

"Understand what?" That came out just as bitchy as the other words.

"What I said to your ex."

He said a bunch of shit to my ex. "Which part?" Gah! I'm so angry with this guy. I mean, the last time he was here, he was a big-time jerk. Then there was no word from him forever. And now? Now he suddenly reappears but it isn't until Quinn blabs to him about Dylan. How am I supposed to believe any of this is real?

"The part where I told him about you and me."

"You and me," I deadpan. Then I laugh. "You and me." Sure, I'm repeating the same words, but I'm incredulous. "There's no 'you and me,' Luke."

"There wasn't, but there is now."

He's so damn close. His breath is skimming over my cheek, and I'm doing my best not to let it go to my head because the man makes me dizzy. "You're only here because Quinn told you about Dylan. You would never have come here on your own, so everything you're saying is utter bullshit."

"What Quinn told me is only part of the reason I finally pulled my head out of my ass. The other part...." I watch as his expression softens. His hand moves up, and a finger skims over my cheek. "I missed you, babe. I felt it here." He places a palm on his chest, over his heart. "The second you walked into the room this morning, I felt like I could breathe again."

Oh. Well, damn. "Luke." It comes out as a whisper.

"Yeah. I know." He chuckles. "I became a pussy."

Okay. He ruined it. Go figure.

Growling in disgust, I press my palms on his chest. I push, hard. But he doesn't budge.

"What?"

"You're a dick. You ruined a perfectly good moment."

"How?" His voice just got higher.

I push again, but it only makes him press closer. "Having feelings doesn't make you a pussy, dickface."

Scoffing, he takes one of my hands and places it on the bed, beside my head. "I know." He sighs. "Look, Tayler, I'm not used to this shit. Cut me some slack. I'm doing what you wanted. I'm here. I'm ready."

"Ready? For what?" *Oh, this ought to be good.*

"To try."

I wait for more, but the guy isn't giving it up. "To try what?" God. He's so damn frustrating. "Spit it out, Luke."

"Us. I'm ready to try."

I blink rapidly. "Us?"

"Us."

My voice sounds strange. Scratchy. "As in not just friends?"

"Friends. With benefits. Exclusive benefits."

I've been straining my neck to look up at him. With those words, however, I let my head flop back onto the bed. I also lose all the fight left in my limbs. Now I'm as limp as a noodle. "Friends with exclusive benefits." It's not a question.

"Yeah." Jesus, he sounds so smug.

Lifting my head, I glare at him. "You know what that means, right?"

"Yeah?" I can tell by his expression that I've confused him with my question. "It means we're friends who fuck but only each other."

"Do I look like the kind of girl who fucks her friends?" I mean... he cannot be serious.

This time, instead of trying to push him off me, I roll to my right and am almost able to get out from beneath him, but he's quick.

"Babe."

I growl and do my best not to knee him in the nuts. It'd serve him right.

"Tayler. Come on."

I give up. He's too close for me to wiggle out, so I'll just stop. But he's got me so frigging pissed. And sad.

So damn sad.

I do that thing I did before. I cry. Not on purpose. It's just it's barely ten in the morning and it's been a shitstorm already. It's Saturday. I was looking forward to spending a lazy morning hanging out with Quinn. We planned on going to the mall later so she could find something cute to wear when Cooke gets here, but now that's not gonna happen. No, now I've got Luke wanting to screw me like I'm a harlot, I've got Dylan stalking me, and on top of all that, I have to go to the police station later. So yeah, I'm crying.

Sue. Me.

"Tayler. Honey." Luke's voice is soft and kind of sweet.

I don't listen to him, though. This isn't about him, necessarily.

"Babe, please stop. I'm sorry."

That sounded nice too, but it doesn't change a damn thing.

"Goddamn it." When he says it, though, he doesn't sound angry. It's more frustrated.

Again, not my problem.

I feel his hand touch my cheek. He uses his finger to nudge my chin up so I'm looking at him. "Honey. Please stop. I can't take you being upset."

I roll my eyes but keep crying. I want to tell him to get used to it, but I can't talk yet. My nose is running, and I bet I look like bloody hell, as Cooke Thompson might say.

When I feel his lips touch mine, my crying stops immediately. New thoughts are running through my head now. When his mouth leaves mine, I reach up and place my hands on his face to pull it back down, and *I* kiss *him*—and I mean I *really* kiss him. I know my wet cheeks are now getting him all wet, but I don't care. When I open my mouth and our tongues meet, I can't believe how good it feels. I wrap my arms and legs around him holding on tight. His body presses down against mine while his fingers weave into my hair.

It's amazing.

It's hotter than our first kiss. Our lips are sealed together, tongues battling for dominance. Our bodies are melded together. God, I wish we were naked. That'd make this so much better.

I feel his dick against me, and I shift my hips upward so I can really feel it. Luke moans first, but I'm not far behind.

"Fuck," he hisses as he pulls his mouth away. I whimper a little, but he's not stopping this. His lips touch my cheek, then my neck, and down the side to my shoulder. I also feel warm skin on my stomach; his hand has found its way into my oversized tee, and I'm grateful for it. His hand moves up fast until it's on top of my left breast. Once there, he squeezes and says, "Fucking amazing tits," in a deep husky voice.

"Thanks," I say fast, then "Pinch my nipple."

"Jesus." Luke's mouth finds mine again for a hungry, deep kiss while his finger and thumb pinch me like I asked. He did it right. Just hard enough. God, I'm wet. So freaking wet I can feel it. I want his hands, his everything. I reach down between us so I can get a feel for him when something terrible happens.

Someone knocks on my door.

We both suddenly stop what we're doing, and I want to cry again in frustration.

"Tayler?" Quinn's voice is soft. "Um... Gage needs to leave."

Luke and I stare at one another. He smiles first, and then me. "Okay. We'll be out in a minute," I call out. As soon as I can get my body under control.

I push on his chest a little, but he takes my hands in his. He's still pressed up against me when he says, "I changed my mind."

I'm not sure I want to hear this. "About?"

"Us."

I feel my eyes burn again and attempt to pull away from him.

"Let me finish. Jesus." Luke's voice sounds cranky.

I stop moving for now. "So finish."

"Wish I could," he mumbles. Looking into my eyes, he leans down and kisses my lips softly. "There's something here." He pauses. "With you and me."

"Chemistry."

"That's part of it. I'd like to see where this goes." Luke swallows so loudly that I hear it. "But you've got to cut me some slack, Tayler. I may not be able to do it. Relationships and me... they don't take."

Oh. My. God. He said "relationship." I want to squeal with delight, but I can't speak right this second, so I just nod. And smile. My smile is huge.

"And we need to finish what we started. Tonight."

I nod quickly. "Tonight."

"My place. Bring your shit to stay over."

"Tonight." I'm staying overnight with Luke Green. At his house. *Holy shit.*

"Come to the bar around nine and we'll head over there together."

"Sure." I lean up again and kiss him. It takes less than a second for the kiss to turn into the one earlier.

Then there's another knock on my door.

Stupid Quinn.

"Fuck," I grumble.

"Tonight, babe. I'm sinking my cock so deep...."

I gasp at his words. They're so damn dirty. I love it.

I smile. "Can't wait."

CHAPTER NINETEEN

Luke

She can't wait.

Fuck. I'm screwed. I nearly came when she asked me to pinch her nipple. Goddamn. Maybe I've met my match. It doesn't seem possible that fucking elegant and gorgeous Tayler Sorenson likes it a little dirty in the sack. If that's the case, I'm either the luckiest man on earth or I'm...

Yeah, I'm screwed.

"Hey," she says from behind me.

When I turn around, her face is flushed a soft pink, and she's smiling. It's not a big smile, but it's enough.

"Hey." My smile, on the other hand, is wide. I haven't stopped thinking about this morning. Not for one second. Hell, just the sight of her makes my dick harden. It's always been like that, but now that I know what's in store for us tonight, it's harder than usual. "Give me ten." I nod to the stool at the end of the bar. "Gotta finish up some shit."

"Sure." She pulls the seat out and sits.

I wonder if she brought a bag with her. I hope so. I told her to, but she's not the kind of woman who takes orders, so we'll see.

I rush through the few things I needed to finish and let my crew know I'm taking off, then round the end of the bar and reach for her hand. Tugging her off the stool, I keep hold of her and walk out the front door. It's cold outside; fall changed to winter overnight, it seems. I peek over at Tayler and see she's wearing a jacket. I can't tell what she's got on under it since she never took it off at the bar, but I can see jeans and sneakers. It makes me smile knowing she didn't go overboard with the clothes. It's not really a date, so why would she?

I walk Tayler to her car. "Meet me at my place."

"Okay."

After I listen for her car to start, I jog back up the street and down an alley to a small lot behind Cy's. Jumping into my car, I start it up and back out slowly. It's a tight space to park behind the bar, and sometimes people smoke out here. I don't like it, but what am I gonna do? I make the drive home in five minutes. When I pull into the driveway, Tayler's car is already parked at the curb. When she starts to slide out of her vehicle, I point to the spot next to mine. "Park here, babe." So her car won't be out on the street all night.

"Oh. Okay."

She slides back in and parks next to me. When she emerges, she's got a purse and a smallish bag with her. It's large enough to hold what she needs to stay a night, maybe two.

Reaching out, I take the bag out of her hand, place it in my left one, and take her hand in my right. I can't believe how good it feels to hold this girl's hand.

"Come on." I lead her to the door, unlock it, and then hold it for her to go first. It's chilly, so I walk over to the thermostat and turn it up, then take the bag into my bedroom and set it on the bed. Turning, I see she's followed me. "You hungry?"

She shakes her head.

"Thirsty?"

"Sure." She smiles. "Water would be good."

"Right." I step past her and reach for her hand, squeezing it as I go. Jesus, I'm fucking nervous. Something I haven't felt since my teens.

I grab two glasses and fill them with water, then drop a couple cubes of ice in each glass as well. I open the fridge and contemplate taking something to eat. Sure, she said she wasn't hungry, but I can tell she's feeling the nerves too. I search the drawers for something, but all I've got are eggs, butter, and an old head of lettuce. "I need to go to the damn store."

I do the same thing in the cupboard. When I find a box of crackers, I grab it hoping they aren't stale.

With the two glasses of water and the box of old crackers, I walk quickly back to my bedroom. The second I'm over the threshold, my throat goes dry because she's sitting on the side of my bed, her legs crossed and her hands resting in her lap. She looks sweet and demure, except for the fact that she's taken off her clothes and what remains is the fucking sexiest bra and panties I've ever seen. They look to be dark green, which is perfect with her pale skin and red hair. The bra—what there is of it—reveals two plump breasts. I've touched one, but I haven't gotten to see them until now.

"Tayler." My voice is raspy. Swallowing, I realize I'm still holding the water and crackers. "Water?" I hold one glass out to her.

Tayler stands, and my eyes drift down her body. Onto those panties. Like the bra, there isn't much to them. There are green ribbons at her hips and a small triangle of green on the front. I'm dying to see beneath, but I need to get my shit together before then.

"Turn around."

Where the hell did that come from?

She stops her approach, and pink flushes over her chest. It's stunning to watch. When she slowly turns, I stare at the ribbon detail and hold my breath as the ribbons meet in the back. It's a thong and it's sexy as fuck, but it's her ass that has me shaking. For such a small girl, she's got a plump little ass. I knew she did—I'd seen it in those tight legging things—but seeing all that beautiful skin for myself? Well, let's just say my dick hurts.

"Take them off. Slow."

So I don't miss a thing, I set the water glasses on my dresser and toss the crackers behind me. I watch as she slips her thumbs into the ribbons pushing down the tiny scrap of lace. When they're just past her knees, they fall the rest of the way down. Tayler kicks them away, then turns to face me. I'm staring at her pussy. I half expected her to be bare, but she's not. She's got a small strip of red hair there, and I'm glad. I like the feel of the curls. I wiggle my fingers, anticipating how they'll feel. Soft. I know they'll be soft.

I stare. I need more. "You wet for me?" I want to know if she's as turned on as I am.

Tayler's voice is husky, sexy. "So wet."

Fuck, I need to get myself under control before I embarrass myself. "The bra. Take it off."

"Bossy," she grumbles, but she reaches back behind her. When she's got it unhooked, the straps fall from her shoulders. With both hands, she pulls the bra away and holds it out in front of me, then lets it drop to the floor.

Her tits are perfect. I know how they fill my hand now, but seeing them, pink and flushed with dusty rose nipples, is taking my breath away.

"On the bed," I say as I reach behind me to pull off my tee. I've got my jeans off and kicked into the corner in no time. All that's left are my briefs. Slipping my fingers into the waistband, I push them down over my rock-hard cock and off, kicking them to the side. As I move closer to the bed, her eyes are on me. Well, on my dick. I know I've got a decent-sized dick, but from the look on her face, I'm guessing I'm a surprise.

"Gonna fuck you hard and fast at first, I'll take my time on round two. That okay with you?"

I watch her swallow, and then she nods. "Yeah."

I reach for her leg and pull her to the edge of the bed. Running my palms up the sides of her thighs to her waist, I move one hand down to her curls and skim my palm over her mound. So soft. "Can't wait to taste you." I say it out loud, but I'm really talking to myself.

"Me too."

My eyes move up from her pussy to her chest, my hands following. When I've got one tit in each hand, I squeeze and run my fingers over the hard tips. I pinch both at the same time, making her moan. Her back arches and her legs open wider.

"Your tits are sensitive."

"Yeah. I love to have them played with."

"Ever had anyone fuck them?" *Please say no.*

She shakes her head sort of shyly. "No."

"We'll do that. You'll love it." And so will I.

Leaning down, I kiss her hard. I'm not going to last, so I need to get this going. Reaching for her hand, I pull her up to stand in front of me, then turn her around. "Hop back up on the bed, hands and knees."

"You really are just gonna fuck me the first time, huh?"

Shit. Is she pissed about that? "I'll make it up to you. Promise."

Tayler laughs, and I feel relieved.

She crawls up on the bed, resting on her hands and knees, giving me the perfect view of that ass of hers. Leaning down, I kiss both of her cheeks. "Stellar ass, babe."

She laughs again.

I slide my hand through her center. She wasn't lying. She's wet as fuck. I find her clit and use my middle finger to swirl around it.

I want to get a feel for her; I want to know what makes her feel good. When her ass begins to move with me, back and forth, I know I'm on to something. "Feel good?" I press a finger inside while still massaging her clit.

"God, yes."

We've got a rhythm now. I slide a second finger inside of her and begin to work her fast. I want to hear her lose it for me before I sink into her. Her breathing is getting louder, as are her moans. She's sexy as fuck.

Leaning over her, I kiss and then bite down on her neck. "Pinch your nipples."

Pushing herself up a little, she uses both hands to find her breasts. I watch her slide them over her hard tips before she squeezes each globe. When she pinches down, I feel her squeezing around my fingers. I also hear her. It's the sexiest sound I've ever heard. "So hot, baby."

I don't want to lose the momentum, so I pull my hand from her and gently nudge her forward onto her hands again. Reaching into my nightstand, I retrieve a condom. Sliding it down quickly, I run my palms over her ass, then up to her waist. Lining myself up, I whisper, "You ready?"

"Yes. God. Fuck me, Luke."

Music to my ears. I press in hard and fast and nearly pass out from the feeling. Euphoria. That's the best word for this. She feels better than the fantasies I had about her. Far better.

Grasping her hips, I pull out fast and plunge right back in. My orgasm is already working its way up my spine. I need to last a little longer than this. Next time.

"Touch your clit, Tayler."

Her finger skims my dick as I piston in and out of her. When she begins to squeeze my cock, I'm a goner. "Fuck." I come so hard and so fast that I feel I need to apologize. Later. Right now, I want to remember this feeling. My head is dizzy, my breathing labored. There's sweat running down my face from my hairline, and I'm wiped out, but it's the best kind of fatigue.

"That was fast but—"

"I know." She laughs. "You'll take your time next time."

I pull out and feel a sense of loss I can't explain. "Give me thirty minutes and I'll show you rather than tell you."

Tayler moves away, turning so she can sit on my bed. "Thirty minutes?"

"Sorry. It takes me a bit." I begin to roll off the condom as I walk toward the hallway.

"No." She giggles. "That's not what I meant. So, you can do it more than once a night?"

Before I'm out the door to dispose of the condom, I turn back to look at her. Now I get what she meant. "I'll fuck you all night long. You want that?"

Her skin flushes again, and I swear my dick starts right back up. She notices it too, making her get even pinker. "I... uh... didn't know." She stares at my dick. "Can all guys...?"

I want to laugh at her question, but from her expression, she's serious. She wants to know. "I haven't asked about it, but I suspect everyone is different."

"Oh. Right." She pauses. "Dylan could only—"

I hold up my hand to stop her. "Please do not talk about another guy when we're about to fuck."

She finally looks at my face. "Are we about to fuck. Again?" She looks down at my dick. "I thought you said you need thirty minutes."

I look down at my erect dick, then back at her. "Give or take."

Her smile is sexy and just a little smug. I love it. "I'll take, please."

I nod, then step out of the room to dispose of the condom. I'd love to know if she's on the pill. We'd have to get tested, but nothing sounds better than going bare with Tayler Sorenson.

CHAPTER TWENTY

Tayler

Three times. That's how many times Luke Green did the kinds of things I've only read about. Having sex with him is like having sex with a professional. LOL. Okay, that's not what I meant. It was like a master class in *the sex*. Compared to Dylan... well, let's just say I didn't know what I was missing. Now that I do, though, I'll never be able to unsee it or undo it again. If things don't work out between Luke and me, I may have to get some cats. Just sayin'.

His voice is soft, "You awake?"

Luke sleeps funny. Like half on his stomach, half on his side. I'm a back sleeper, so most of the time we actually slept, he had one of his arms flung over my middle. He pulled me in until my hip was touching something of his. Ordinarily, I'd prefer to sleep on my own side of the bed, but something about Luke makes me crave his skin touching mine. Maybe it's due to the fact that the guy has walls so this... well, this feels intimate, private, personal.

"I'm awake."

He rolls to his back, pulling me along with him. By the time he's on his back, I'm half on top of the guy. I spot it immediately. He's hard again. My goodness, the man is a machine. "Again?"

His big warm palm is on my lower back, right above my ass. Or it was. Now it's sliding down over one cheek, then back up my spine to my neck. Repeat. Damn, it feels amazing. He's doing it so slowly, and it's making me warm all over. Laying my head down on his chest, I use my own hand to do something similar to him, only to his front. I let my hand discover all of the ridges of his abs. He's got a glorious body. He should volunteer as a model for the life drawing classes at the design college. They'd have a field day with his bod.

I follow the line of blond hairs down to his thick, long dick. The second I slide my palm down the length, it bobs and grows even more.

"Babe." Luke's palm is still moving, but since I've been touching him, it's been mostly on my butt. He squeezes one of my cheeks and I squeak. "You gonna put your mouth on me or what?"

I peer up at his face and smirk. "You want my mouth on you?" I pump my hand up and slide my thumb over the head.

With a deep groan, he says, "More than you'll ever know."

I adjust my body so I'm right above his cock. Lowering, I look up at him as I swipe my tongue over the head.

"Tayler." It comes out as a hiss, and it propels me on.

I taste him, then smile as Luke's hips jump up from the bed just a little. Dylan loved getting head. However, I didn't enjoy doing it. Not to him, anyway. Doing this with Luke is a different story. For one thing, Dylan never reciprocated. Ever. But since Luke already did that during round two of *the sex*, then it's only fair. Besides, hearing a man like Luke Green hiss your name is something to behold.

I lick his shaft from the base to the head again, moaning a little myself. It's empowering, this effect I'm having on the man. At the top, I wrap my lips around him and use my tongue at the base of the head.

"Jesus, fuck," Luke says, gritting his teeth. "Do that again."

I don't do exactly that. Instead, I remove my mouth and lick from the bottom up again, then wrap my hand around him and pump up and down twice. With my mouth around him again, I press down as far as I can go, which isn't far (I don't have deep-throat skills) and suck as I move back up. I feel Luke's palm that was on my ass move down to my crease. My turn to moan.

"You're so fucking wet. You like sucking my cock?"

I moan again, and he rewards me with his fingers. One and then two inside, pumping in the same rhythm as my mouth. I love it. I'm close to climax when he removes his fingers. I quickly lift my head in protest. I blink when he attempts to lift me by the hips.

"Straddle my face," he says like it's an order.

Adjusting, I find myself doing something I never, not in my wildest imagination, thought I'd do. That's right, ladies and gents, I'm 69-ing with Luke fucking Green. His hands are back on my hips, pulling me closer to his face. I should probably cringe imagining what I must look like from that vantage point, but I'm too turned on to care. The second his tongue touches my clit, I arch my back and give him my own hiss. "Yesss...."

"Suck my cock, babe."

Returning to my task, I feel more urgency than I did before. I'm still chasing my orgasm, but I do my best to concentrate. Once we get that rhythm going again, I crack first. Still unable to do two things at once, I throw my head back and practically scream as the orgasm hits me.

"Holy shit," I say with a laugh.

Before I know it, Luke's got his hands beneath my arms and I'm being lifted and turned to face him, my knees on either side of his hips. I guess we're doing it this way. "Lift up."

I push up as he positions himself at my center. I stare down at his cock. "Condom?"

"Fuck." Reaching to his right and opening his nightstand drawer, he fishes around for a few seconds and cusses again.

Rolling, he leans over the drawer and cusses again. "Motherfucker."

"You out?"

With a sigh, he flops back onto the bed. "I don't suppose you're on birth control."

I nod. I am.

We stare at each other for what feels like a solid ten minutes, but it was probably more like one. "I'm not comfortable...." I mean, the guy is sort of a slut. Or he was. How do I know if he's always worn protection? Take right now, for example. He's ready to go condom-free with me and it's our first night.

"I've only ever gone bare with one other person."

"One person?" *Who was she?* I'm dying to ask, but I don't.

He nods.

Dylan and I quit using condoms after the first year. It was a risk, but I thought I was going to marry the ass. It doesn't feel right with Luke, though. Not yet. "I, uh, think we should get tested before we do something like that."

"Agreed."

Still up on my knees, I look down at his hard dick. Reaching down, I wrap my hand around him, then look up at him. He gives me his trademark smirk, and I do what I need to do to make sure he gets his happy ending.

CHAPTER TWENTY-ONE

Luke

Sex with Tayler is better than I imagined. It's a revelation, honestly. She's the complete package: confident, assertive, and demure. And bundle that up with the fact that her body is killer. She doesn't have the kind of body that screams "I work out"; instead, it's soft and a little round in all the right places. Not only that, the girl has freckles *everywhere*. It may be the biggest turn-on of all, and that surprises me. I found myself wanting to use my tongue on her like I was drawing a connect-the-dots picture. There are thousands of them, so you can imagine how much fun that'd be. And between each dot is porcelain skin. She looks like a tapestry, and it's beautiful.

When we woke up the next morning, I made her breakfast, which we ate on my living room couch. She helped me clean up, and then things got awkward. I don't ordinarily do sleepovers and definitely not at my place, so I wasn't sure if I should take her back to bed or hint for her to go home. Honest to fuck, I wasn't sure I could do it again that morning. The woman wore me out. But looking at her in her tiny pajama shorts and tank, I was willing to go again. I'd have time to recover later.

But she did us both a favor, and as soon as the dishes were done, she told me she needed to get home. She had homework.

I breathed a little sigh of relief, but she couldn't see it. It was all inside. I gave her a quick kiss and promised to call her. That was two days ago. I know I need to call her, so I do the next best thing.

Me: Hey

I don't have to wait long.

Forever Girl: Hey

That's it? She's not gonna give me more than "Hey"? Now what? Do I need to say more? Shit. I have no idea what the fuck I'm doing.

Me: What's up?

Forever Girl: Same old.

Same old? WTF? I don't know her well enough to know what "Same old" even means.

Me: Gonna give me more than that?

Forever Girl: Are you?

Mother....

Me: My head hurts.

Forever Girl: Oh? Are you okay?

No.

Me: I'm sure it'll go away.

Eventually.

Forever Girl: Do you have aspirin or something?

Me: Yeah. Took some.

Forever Girl: Can I do anything?

Yes. You can show up in nothing but a coat. But I suppose that's friends-with-benefits territory, and we know how she feels about that.

Me: Nah.

Forever Girl: You sure?

Me: Yep. Need to get ready for work.

Forever Girl: Feel better.

Me: Talk to you later.

Forever Girl: Sure.

Sure? What does she mean by that? If I'd called her, I could have heard the tone of her voice. Then I'd know if she was pissed or not.

Forever Girl: Let me know if you need anything. Seriously.

Me: Will do.

I won't, but now that I know she's not pissed, I think my headache is dissipating. A little, anyway.

My headache is back.

Yeah, I know. You don't need to say it. I've let too much time pass between the last texts with Tayler and today. A week, to be exact. I know I told her I'd "talk to her later," and I meant it, but the more days that passed, the more hesitant I was to call because I know she's probably upset now. I would be.

So, I've been focused on the bar. Since Quinn hasn't been around at all, I need to hire at least one more bartender. Adding a waitress to the mix would be helpful too but hiring someone right now will be difficult since the holidays are right around the corner. Students like to head home for Thanksgiving and for the three or four weeks off between the fall and spring semesters, so I need to find someone who's gonna be around. My first thought is Tayler, but I'm not sure what her plans are for the holidays and I don't want to go there.

When the front door to the bar opens, I look up and see one big motherfucker walk through the door on a pair of crutches. I recognize him immediately due to the fact that his girl, Quinn, is behind him. Not only that, he's got the most fucked-up brace on his leg I've ever seen. Stepping around the bar, I hold my hand up to shake his. "What the hell, man?" I bend to get a closer look. The metal brace reminds me of scaffolding you'd see on the outside of a building. "That looks like the same kind of thing they used on the Redskins quarterback last year."

"Aye," he says in his British accent. "Same concept."

"Shit." It looks painful as hell. "Sorry, man."

Our conversation is interrupted by "I'm here to get my check."

I turn and see Quinn standing next to Cooke. Her lips are pursed like she's tasted some lemons. I bet I'm the bad lemon in this scenario. "Sure. In the office. I'll get it for you." I attempt a smile, but it produces no response from Quinn, and I know why. This is all about Tayler. "You two want a drink?"

"Aye." Cooke smiles as he places his crutches in one hand, then hops on his good leg up to the bar. "Guinness, lad."

Lad? We're probably the same age.

"Quinn?" She's moved up to help Cooke. Once he's settled, she sits next to him.

"Water," she replies.

I grab her a bottled water from the cooler and pour the beer. Setting them on the bar, I excuse myself to get her check. I'm tempted to ask her what's up with Tayler, but I have a feeling I won't have to say anything. She'll do all the talking. Quinn's like that. She can't keep shit bottled in. I respect that, even though I'm not really in the mood to get my ass chewed by one of my employees.

When I return, I set the check on the bar and wait. When she doesn't say anything, I offer something from the kitchen.

"I could eat," Cooke says, looking over at Quinn. "You hungry, love?"

She doesn't answer. Instead, she turns her icy glare to me. "What the ever-loving hell is wrong with you, Luke Green?"

And there it is.

I shrug. "Lots of shit wrong with me, Quinn."

"You tell our girl you want to give your relationship a try and then you don't call her for a frigging week?"

I nod. What can I say to that?

"You can't do that." She turns to Cooke. "Would you do that? Would you tell someone that, *sleep* with them, then not call?"

"Love," Cooke says softly. "You know I wouldn't. The second I get this blasted thing off my leg, you're never leaving my bed."

Okay. TMI.

I watch as Quinn's face turns a bright pink color. I want to laugh, but I know that wouldn't end well.

She turns back to me. "See? A *real* man doesn't do that kind of thing."

"Hey!" I take offense to that. I'm a real man.

"No. You don't get to defend yourself on that one. Have you wondered how she is? Are you worried that Dylan's reappeared?"

"Has he?" Fuck.

"You don't get to ask that question. Not to me. Did you wonder if he wrote her another creepy letter?"

"Did he?"

She holds up her hand. "Maybe he did. Maybe he didn't. If he did, we gave it to Gage. *He'll* take care of her."

"The fuck?" I spit. "Gage?"

"What of it?" Quinn snaps back. "He's called her almost every day to check on her. But have you?"

I lay my head back and stare at the ceiling. "Quinn—"

"No. And don't you dare call her now. If she finds out I came here and told you that, she'll kill me. And if she kills me, I'm going to tell Cooke to hobble over to Cy's and punch you in your damn junk."

Cooke chuckles. "No, Love. His throat. Punch him in his throat. I want nuttin' to do with his junk."

"Whatever," she snaps at her man. "It's the punching part that matters."

"Aye." Cooke sips his beer. I guess my expression isn't pleasing him, because he sets his glass down slowly and grunts, "And don't look so smug, lad. Even with this brace, I'll kick your bloody ass."

I have my doubts about that, but I'm keeping my mouth shut. He is a professional athlete, after all, so I just nod.

"Look, Quinn—"

"No," she snaps, holding up her hand to stop me from speaking. "I don't know who screwed you up, but you can't treat Tayler like this. Either shit or get off the pot. If you like her and want to see where it goes, you can't ghost her for a week and expect things to be hunky-dory."

"Time got away from me. I...." I stop when Quinn rolls her eyes.

"You're a grown-ass man. You own your business. Time doesn't get away from *you*, Luke. That's bullshit."

She's right. "I let too much time pass. The longer it went, the more I worried she'd be mad."

"Here's some advice. Don't do that." She throws up her hands. "God, all you had to do was text her, you idiot."

"Right." She's right. A quick text would have done it. God, my head hurts.

Sliding off her seat, Quinn reaches around Cooke to grab his crutches. "I like you, Luke. I even like you for Tayler, but she can't take this crap from you. She needs to focus on school, and you're messing with her head. That's not fair to her."

"Does she still need a job?"

What the fuck am I doing?

"She needs something over break."

"I need help over break."

"Well then, I guess you'd better talk to her. Be honest with her about why you didn't call. No games. Be a damn grown-up."

I nod, hoping Quinn leaves soon. I can't take her lecturing me much longer.

Cooke quickly drinks the rest of his beer and reaches into his pocket for his wallet. I wave him off. "On the house."

With a shrug he reaches for his crutches. Once he's set, he turns to me. "Later, Luke."

"Later."

CHAPTER TWENTY-TWO

Tayler

I blink at my phone, then scoff. *Now* he texts?

Luke: Hey, babe.

I've got a myriad of emotions running through my mind right now. First, I'm angry. A week has passed, and that's the text he finally chooses to send? It's sad. Sad that it took him a week to reach out. But I'm relieved. I'm tired of thinking about him, and I'm tired of wondering what's going on between the two of us.

I decide to ignore it rather than get into a pissing match with him about the reasons why he's such a dick. I need to focus on my final project, but I haven't been able to concentrate long enough to put anything together. So, now that he's sent me a message, I'm determined to let Luke stew on it for a while.

Pulling out my fabric swatches, I curl up on my couch and begin to work through my ideas. Not fifteen minutes later, my phone chimes. I squeeze my eyes shut, willing myself not to look, but my curiosity gets the best of me.

Luke: I know you're angry.

Oh really? He *knows* I'm angry? How could he? He's been MIA for a week. God, I'm definitely pissed. Screw the other emotions.

Sucking in a deep breath, I decide to ignore that text as well. I was finally getting something done.

Luke: The thing is, the longer I waited, the harder it was.

What the eff?

Luke: So I decided to risk it.

Risk it? Why can't the guy just apologize? It's like he's unable to do the common sense thing.

Luke: I can tell you're not going to respond, so I'm going to keep going.

Luke: Have you heard from your stalker?

I can't even....

Luke: Let me know.

Luke: Hey, I need help at the bar over break. You interested?

I can't do this. I can't keep staring down at my phone waiting for his next message. I've got work to do. Although, I do need a job. I'll find one too—just not at Cy's Roost. Pressing the power button on the phone, I watch the screen go black.

I wish I could tell you that it made me feel better, but it didn't. All it did was make me constantly wonder what else he wrote. So, cutting my losses, I turn it back on.

Luke: I'm gonna let you do what you need to do until I get home from work. Then I'm calling you. I hope you pick up the phone. We need to talk.

We need to talk?

Four words that hold so much meaning—and create so much doubt.

I hate those four words.

My phone rings at two in the morning. When his name flashes across the screen, I sigh and pick up my phone because I'm a damn glutton for punishment, and also because I can't get "We need to talk" out of my head.

"Hello?"

"I'm downstairs. Can you come let me in?"

Our landlord, Vic, finally put a secure lock on the front door after my ordeal with Dylan. To say the other tenants of the building were unhappy is an understatement, but Vic's words are final around here, and everyone's been doing a decent job making sure the door's locked up.

"You're here?" Damn. I wasn't expecting him to stop by.

"It's cold, babe."

"I'll be down." *As soon as I brush my teeth, hair, and change into a shirt that doesn't have ketchup stains on it.*

I rush through those things as fast as I can. Making sure I don't lock myself out, I place a shoe in the door and race down to the first floor. I see him right away, his warm breath causing steam to float out around his head. Flipping the lock on the door, I open it and stand aside. A second later, I'm pressed against the wall next to the door, his lips on mine. Hungry, fervent lips. I know I should be angry, should push him away, but my God, this man makes me feel things I've only dreamt about. So I do what feels right: I wrap myself around him and welcome him.

"Fuck, Tayler." Luke moans into my neck. "I've missed you. I'm sorry I'm so bad at this shit." When his cold hand finds its way beneath my clean tee, I squeak in surprise. "Sorry, babe."

I'm not sorry.

His chilly fingers find my breast, and I press into him. I like the sensation of the cold on my warm skin. "Yeah," I say breathlessly. "We could have been doing this all week if you hadn't been such a stubborn idiot."

I feel his body shake against mine. Is he laughing? He pulls his head back from my neck, and the smile on his face tells me that, yes, he's laughing. The man doesn't smile much, but when he does, it's stunning. Luke's got straight white teeth surrounded by lush, full lips. "Want to go upstairs?"

"Fuck yes."

Taking him by the hand, I lead him up one flight, then pause on the first landing and turn to kiss him again. This time, both of his hands find my ass. He squeezes my cheeks hard, and I like it. Luke then lifts me up, and I wrap my legs around his middle as he carries me up the rest of the way to my apartment.

"Bedroom," I say into his ear.

"Way ahead of you."

Before I know it, I'm on my back on my bed, and Luke is tearing off his clothes. I stare for a bit, watching the show. That is until he growls, "Get naked."

Wow, I love how damn dominant he is. Slipping off my shirt, I toss it onto the floor, then wiggle out of my sleep shorts and panties in time to watch Luke do the same. Moments later, I've got my legs wrapped around his waist, and his mouth is on my breast.

"So beautiful, Tayler."

I can barely speak. Not when he's doing that with his tongue. "Thanks. Now, will you fuck me already?" It's been a week, but it feels longer.

"Hell yeah."

Luke uses his hand to adjust us just right. When he slams home, my toes curl, and I yell some unintelligible things. Nothing has ever felt this good.

"Not gonna last."

I don't care as long as he keeps pounding into me like he is. I love this animal-like way of doing it. My climax comes out of nowhere, surprising me. I'm pulsing around him as he adjusts my legs so they're on his shoulders. Pushing up onto his knees, he brings my hips closer so he can get even deeper. How can it be?

"Jesus, so good." Luke's muttering all sorts of things while he pistons in and out of me. A second orgasm is right around the corner when he says, "Gonna fill you up."

It's then I remember. "No. No condom." I stare up at him.

I must look terrified, because he pulls out suddenly and comes all over my stomach. "Shit, Tayler. I'm sorry." He sets my legs down onto the bed gently, reaches for his discarded shirt, and wipes off my belly. "Fuck. I'm sorry. We talked about this. I'm sorry."

"No. It's okay." It's not, but it takes two people.... "We'll get tested." I look up at him. "Right?"

He nods. "This week. I'll make us both appointments."

"I'll go to student health. They do free screenings."

"Right. Good."

I can tell he's regretting it, though I don't know if it's because of the whole STD thing or pregnancy.

"I'm on birth control. I won't get pregnant, if that's what you're worried about."

Luke won't look at me, his eyes are still on my stomach. "No." He shakes his head, then stops. "Maybe." He slides off the bed and retrieves my tee. Tossing it onto the bed, he bends to pick up his briefs, giving me a good glimpse of his muscled ass. "I'd better take off."

"You're leaving?" Okay, if he leaves right now, after that, I'm going to be majorly pissed off. I'm not going to play these stupid games with this man.

"You want me to stay?" His voice practically squeaks. "After I did that?" He points at my belly again.

"It's three in the damn morning." And we're supposed to be in a relationship. "If you leave now, I can't do this with you."

"Can't do what?"

Sliding off the bed, I grab the tee and throw it over my head angrily. "Any of this!" Yeah, I'm yelling. I hope my neighbors can't hear me. "Be a grown-up, Luke. These things happen. We'll deal with it as a *couple*. Running away isn't the way you handle awkward situations like this. If you leave now...."

Luke runs his fingers through his hair. It's shorter than it was a week ago. He must have gotten it cut. "I don't want to leave. I fucked up. I'm sorry."

"Stop." I step closer to him. Taking his hand in mine, I gaze into his eyes. "We'll deal with it. Now, I'm going to get a glass of water. You want some?" I move through my bedroom door toward the kitchen.

"Sure." He says as he follows me out. "Got any food?"

My smile is much broader. "Chips and dip, crackers, things of that nature."

"You've got to have more food than chips and crackers, babe."

I roll my eyes, but he can't see me since my back is to him. "You'll see."

After looking through my cupboards and my fridge, Luke steps up behind me, wrapping his arms around my waist as I make him a peanut butter sandwich. "You weren't kidding. We need to get you some groceries."

We? "It's on my to-do list as soon as I finish up my project. Until then, I'm getting by with what I have."

He's kissing my neck and it tingles. But when he says, "Woman cannot survive on ramen alone, Tayler," I laugh out loud.

"Quinn's the ramen freak. Thankfully, Cooke requires actual food, so she'll eat something decent while she's at his place."

"You need actual food too. We could go in the morning."

"No can do. I've got to get up in—" I look at the clock. "—3.5 hours. I've got an appointment with a dentist's office."

"Shit." He pulls away fast. I hate it. "Let me do that. You get into bed. Turn out the light. I'll be there as soon as I wolf down this sandwich."

"No. I'm done." I hold up his snack. "See?"

"Thanks, babe."

I stare as he eats the thing in less than four bites. "You were hungry."

Chewing, he tries to say, "My head hurt, so I skipped dinner."

I touch his forehead. "What's up with your headaches? Did you go to the doctor?"

"No." He wraps me up again. "You're my cure. It goes away when I'm with you."

Seriously? That's weird, but I refuse to worry him. "That's because I'm good medicine."

"You're the *best* medicine."

I smile up at him but keep quiet. I want those words to linger for a bit.

It doesn't last long, because Luke pats my ass and says, "Off to bed with you."

I turn and start to walk out of the kitchen. Looking back at him, I've got to ask, "You're coming too, right?"

"Right behind you. Gonna use the john first."

I walk into the bedroom and throw back the covers. Scooting in until I'm on the far side of the bed, I glance at the door just as he walks in. "Switch is on the left." I point to the light switch.

He turns it off, and then I feel the bed dip. When he's all the way in, he pulls the covers over us both, then rolls until he's in his weird position. He reaches out and rests his arm on my stomach, pulling me into him. Releasing a sigh that honestly sounds like he's been holding it for days, he whispers, "Missed you."

"Missed you too." More than he'll ever know. With him next to me, my worries over school, over Dylan, about everything sort of float up into the air and dissipate. He does that for me. I wonder if I do that for him.

"Go to sleep. I'll be here when you wake up."

"Okay. Night, Luke."

"Night, angel."

Ooh, *angel*. I like that one.

CHAPTER TWENTY-THREE

Luke

Tayler looks like shit, and it's my fault. She's walking like a zombie around her kitchen. She's made coffee and pulled out the last two pieces of bread, though I'm not sure what she's going to do with the bread because right this second, she's just holding it and staring at her cup of coffee.

"You gonna eat that bread, babe?"

"Oh." She looks up at me and smiles. God, she's beautiful, even this morning with barely any sleep and her long red hair sort of all over the place. Her face gleams this time of the morning. "I was going to make you toast, but I'm out of butter."

"You don't need to make me toast."

"And another thing," she says, looking pretty cross at me. "How can you look this good with practically no sleep?"

I haven't looked in the mirror but I'm guessing I don't have bedhead like she does. I shrug. "Natural good looks?"

"Fuck you," she mutters. "I need to get ready. I'm meeting with Dr. Bushnell and her husband this morning."

"Oh? You mentioned a dentist appointment. Something wrong with your teeth?" And why is she meeting with the husband too?

"No. My final project is to redesign the interior of a commercial property. Part of the assignment is to find a client willing to let me get in there and measure everything, create a design, and maybe even convince them to redo their place. Dr. Bushnell's office is *so* dated." She rolls her eyes. "The 80s were terrible for design."

"Uh-huh." I nod like I know what she's saying. "Well, I'll get out of your hair." I smirk, pointing at her bedhead.

"Fuck you," she grumbles, attempting to run her fingers through the mess on her head.

Standing up, I walk over to her, lean down, and kiss her softly. "Come by the bar later. I've got to work lunch."

Giving me a sleepy smile, she says, "Okay. I'll let you know what the Bushnells say."

"Good. Later, babe."

Coming out of the kitchen with two cheeseburger baskets, I see her sitting at the bar. She doesn't look happy, but I'm swamped, so I can't really take the time to find out what's wrong, though something tells me it has to do with the dentist.

"This place is crazy," she says as I pass her again.

"Yep." I practically jog back into the kitchen, hoping my part-time cook, Zach, has gotten the lead out and caught up.

The second I get back into the kitchen, I see he not only hasn't gotten the lead out, but he's nowhere to be seen. "Zach!" I yell, but not so loud that the customers can hear me. "Zach!" I try again as I make my way out the door that leads to the alleyway behind the bar. I spy him leaning against the wall, smoking. "Fuck, man. Get your ass in here. And I told you not to smoke out here. Jesus, man."

"Sorry," the asshole says, tossing the butt out into the alley. The fucker doesn't even put it out first.

"Put that shit out and pick up the butt."

"Sure, Luke."

I'd like to stay and watch to make sure he does it, but people are going to start rioting if food doesn't get out there.

I stomp back into the kitchen, ready to cook, when I see her standing at the griddle. She's got five or six burgers cooking on the grill and the fryer is going, most likely filled with fries.

"Babe."

I want to reach out and kiss her, but she's busy. And cute in one of my Cy's Roost aprons.

"I used to work at the country club. We had to do everything there."

She shrugs like it's not a big deal. It is, though. To me.

"I'll have these three orders up in a jiffy."

"What the hell, man?" a voice snaps behind me. It's Zach. "You're letting some chick take over my job?"

"That's not just a chick, that's my girl. And yes, she's taking over. Go bus tables and make sure people know their food will be out in a minute."

"Luke, I'm not a fucking busboy," he seethes.

"You are today."

"Fucking bullshit," Zach mutters as he leaves the kitchen.

I move up to the prep table and prepare the baskets for the burgers. "Did you see the chicken strip basket order?" I ask Tayler.

"Yep, in the fryer," she says almost absently.

By the time she's got the meat cooked, I've got the buns ready with the toppings and fries on the side. "I'll be back. Throw some more burgers on, would you?"

"Way ahead of you." And she was. She already had more on the grill.

Giving her a big smile, I set out to deliver the food and spot Zach chitchatting with some women at the bar. If I had time, I'd probably fire the asshole right this second, but that'll have to wait.

"Zach!" I yell. "Bus!"

"I'm doing it," he whines.

Yeah, I'm gonna fire his ass.

CHAPTER TWENTY-FOUR

Tayler

"You're hired."

I turn to smile at Luke as he walks back into the kitchen with a stack of red plastic baskets.

"Oh yeah?"

"Yeah. Besides Chris and Quinn, I've never seen anyone work the way you did just now."

"I'm good," I say, tossing down the towel I used to wipe down the counters. "But you already know that." *Wow, where did all that confidence come from?*

I swear I see Luke blush, and it's the cutest thing ever. "Yeah, you're the best."

Now it's my turn to blush because I think he means it. "You hungry? I made you a triple-stacked burger," I say with a laugh. "I made myself a single."

"I could eat."

"Where's Zach?" The worthless piece of crap.

"Wiping down tables."

"He always like that?"

"Yeah." He nods. "It's another reason I need help around here."

"Apparently," I say with an eyeroll. "However, I'm ordinarily in class at lunch. Today I had a pass because of my meeting this morning." The meeting that wasn't.

"I meant to ask. What happened?"

"Well, Dr. Bushnell couldn't make it, so it was just her husband." He was so smarmy. He kept touching me. I lost count of the number of times he reached out to touch my shoulder, arm, hand, and one time, my knee. It gave me the creeps, which also messed up my presentation. "He had no interest in having me redesign *anything*." Well, he mentioned I could redo his bedroom. Disgusting pervert. "So, it was a waste of time. I even had a preliminary board of samples for him and a rough floor plan." Which I based on the county assessor's information on the building. The prep took hours, but that's fine. It's just part of it. Sometimes clients don't like your work. That's the way it is.

I pick up the baskets, and as I'm about to head out of the kitchen, the door swings open so hard, I jerk back and run into the prep table. The baskets I was holding filled with food for Luke and me are now on the floor.

"Goddamn it, Zach." Luke looks at me with concern. "You okay, Tayler?"

"Yeah." I stare down at my yummy burger. "Sad about the food, though." I'm starving.

"Go sit down. I'll make us up some more while Zach cleans this shit up."

"Me?" he whines again. "She's the one—"

Standing up to his full height, Luke glares at Zach, causing him to stop talking. "Clean it up and clock out."

"But I'm on 'til three."

What is wrong with this kid? He's clueless.

"You're getting off early." Luke's eyes are tiny slits, he looks angry. If I were that guy, I'd take a hint. "And if I walk out into the alley and see that butt on the ground, you're done here."

Zach glances at the back door, then back at Luke. "I'll, uh, double-check."

"Good idea." We both watch Zach skitter out the back door, no doubt to pick up his cigarette. "Babe, go sit. I'll be out in a minute."

"Okay. I'll make sure nobody needs a refill."

"Sure," he says, his back to me. He's already got the meat on the grill.

Out front, the place is nearly deserted, so I sit at the bar and look around. "Now this place could use a redesign." I tap my chin with my index finger. "I wonder...."

"You wonder what?"

I didn't hear him approach, his voice making me jump in my seat. The man is a ninja. "Would you let me use Cy's for my project?"

He looks at me, silent. "It's just pretend, yeah? I've got enough on my plate with my house."

"Sure. It's pretend." I nod. That is until I can convince him to do a few very low-cost changes. The more I can convince him to do, the better my grade will be.

Luke arches his left brow. "I mean it. I'm not changing anything."

"What if I can get your kitchen space working better?" I know I can do that much.

"I'm not committing to anything."

I want to roll my eyes and say "Duh," but I keep my mouth shut. "It's just a design. No worries."

"Fine. Yeah." He sighs, setting my burger down in front of me.

Clapping my hands, I reach out and hug him around the waist. "Yay! I'm so excited."

"Yay," Luke echoes, but it doesn't sound convincing. At. All.

I'll show him how cool it could be in here. I have to.

As I bite into my lunch, I hear him quietly say, "Why do I have the feeling I'm going to regret this?"

I think there's more to those words. He didn't just mean my interior design project, which saddens me, but then again, I'm not the kind of person to give up easily. On anything.

CHAPTER TWENTY-FIVE

Luke

Why did I ever agree to this?

Oh, I know the answer. She swayed me with her work ethic and that sweet pussy of hers. Mostly it was the work ethic, but the pussy was definitely a factor.

Since I agreed to let her "redesign" the bar, she's been in and out of Cy's almost every day. Not only that, she's been picking up shifts for me when I've needed her. Needless to say, we've been spending *a lot* of time together. I'd say there's only been a few nights in the last month that we haven't slept together.

Now, with finals week fast approaching, she surprises me by telling me I need to show up to one of her classes so she can present me with her design—in front of the entire class. And guess what... today's the day.

Did I know this was going to happen?

No, I did not.

Not only that, her professor can't know we're a couple. "It's okay that I work there," she told me, "but my professor will *not* be happy about the fact that we're in a relationship and I need an A on this project. So, just sit there and pretend you have no idea what I've designed."

"I *don't* know what you've designed." I really don't. She's kept it a secret for a month as she's been working like a bee measuring shit and taking pictures.

"Well, I want you to be surprised. Oh, and can you please dress nice?"

I look down at my tee and jeans. It's one of my nice tees and my best pair of jeans. I'm immediately incensed. "What the fuck's wrong with my clothes?"

Here we go.

"Nothing. You look great, but can you slip on a jacket?"

"A jacket?" What the hell is she talking about? "What kind of jacket?"

This ought to be good.

"Um." Her voice is suddenly soft. "A suit jacket?"

I've got one suit. I call it my death suit because I only wear it to funerals. "Tayler," I snap. "Don't fucking start changing me." The truth is, I used to have several suits. Shanna insisted.

"I'm not." Tayler's face has gotten red. "I'm sorry. Wear what you want. How 'bout a sweater?"

I shake my head and walk back into my bedroom, yanking open the bottom drawer of my dresser so hard that the drawer flies all the way out. I don't care. Digging to the bottom, I find a dark blue sweater my mom gave me a bunch of Christmases ago. Once I slip it over my head, I have a hard time getting my arms into it. I've gained quite a bit of muscle since she gave me this.

By the time I've got the stupid thing on, Tayler's followed me into the bedroom and is watching. When she starts to laugh, I've fucking had it.

"Why the fuck are you laughing?"

She immediately stops. "Sorry. It's just...."

"What?"

"That sweater's too small."

I know. I can barely breathe. "You wanted a sweater. This is it. I've got sweatshirts."

"What about a dress shirt?"

I almost rip the sweater getting it off. Stomping over to my closet, I slam the door open and stare inside. She's next to me now and pointing into my closet. "What about this one?"

"It's purple." Another gift from my mom. I swear she thinks I'm a pussy. "I'm not wearing that."

"This one?" She holds up a plaid shirt I've worn a couple of times.

"Fine." I yank it out of her hands. "Fucking bullshit," I mutter.

"God, Luke. What's your problem?"

"My problem?" I glare at her. Her freckled face is red, and there's concern written all over it. I shouldn't be giving her such a hard time, but damn it, I'm not going there with her. "I don't have a problem."

Her hands go to her hips. She's got on a pretty dress for her presentation. Her hair is all done up in a librarian bun—I know it's not called that, but she reminds me of a sexy librarian so I'm going with it. She looks amazing. Hell, she's even got on heels. "Yes you do."

No matter how good she looks, I'm still angry. "Stop trying to change me."

"You know what?" she snaps and starts to leave my room. "Wear whatever the fuck you want, Luke. Wear your pajamas. I don't give two shits. This is only the most important presentation of my college career, but you go ahead and be a little bitch and wear your grubby tee and jeans."

Little bitch?

"I'm not a little bitch. I just don't like it when—"

"Your girlfriend gives you a suggestion on what to wear?"

"Girlfriend?" I'm not ready for labels.

I think I've really shocked her with that question, because her mouth is opening and closing like she'd like to say something. Nothing's coming out, though.

What did she expect? You can't just throw out the G-word like that without consulting a guy.

"I'm.... I've got to go. I'll see you there."

"Hey," I say, following her out of the bedroom. "I thought we were going over together." I don't know where to go once I get to the college.

"Room 584."

I watch her slip on her long coat. Picking up her large portfolio and her backpack, Tayler walks out of my house and to her car without looking back once.

I fucked up. Now what do I do?

But the real question is do I want to do anything?

SHE'S NERVOUS. I've never seen her like this before. Where's the confident girl who walked out on me this morning? This girl, well, I don't recognize her. Her voice is shaky, her skin is blotchy, and I swear her hands are shaking.

I look to her left and see she's got two large boards sitting on easels in the front of the room. One of them has drawings and photos of my bar. Another one has different materials attached to it, like wood for floors, paint swatches, and some metal pieces that look like cabinet hardware. There's also a presentation displayed on the wall in front of her, showing more pictures of the bar and some computer-generated renderings of Cy's before and a bunch showing her new design. In her hand is a small device that she's using to change the images on the wall.

"As you can see, the first thing I've done is eliminate the narthex at the entrance, opening up the space a great deal. With that done, I'm able to move the bar to the opposite side of this main room."

I want to scoff or at least snort. Do you know how much it

would cost to relocate the entire bar? A ton, that's how much. And what the fuck is a narthex?

"By doing so, the kitchen could be enlarged, adding more prep space as well as room for more than one cook at a time." Tayler looks over at me and smiles. I do my best to smile back, but it ain't easy. This plan of hers looks like it'll cost me about a million bucks.

While it would be nice, redoing my kitchen at the bar is not cost-effective, especially since I'd lose money shutting down the restaurant while the work was done.

"I'd reconfigure the booths and tables for more seating, but the thing I'm most excited about is this." She uses the thing in her hand to flip the image to a rendering of an outdoor space.

"By moving the bar, we could add a doorway that leads to the alley adjacent to the building. Since the city has already closed off the alley, it's no longer a thoroughfare, so it's possible to enclose the space, with city approval, to create an outdoor seating area for the bar."

I stare at the screen. The computer-generated image has turned the alley into a courtyard with booths, tables, a small bar, and ivy growing up one of the walls. The Cy's Roost logo is painted on another wall. In a different image, this one from the vantage point of someone sitting in one of the booths, you can see how she used cool outdoor lights to give the place a backyard feel. It's pretty nice, actually.

"What about a fire pit?" I say without thinking.

"That's a good idea," she says with a bright smile. "A fireplace on this brick wall might be better. I can check with the city about that."

"You didn't anticipate that?" asks an older woman dressed in head-to-toe black. I assume she's Tayler's professor.

My girl nods. "I checked with them about a grill, and they said they'd approve it as long as it was natural gas. There's a gas line from the building, so I'd assume a fireplace would also be okay."

"Don't assume," says the bitch in black.

Tayler looks at me, then back at the woman. "Of course not."

Now I can see why she's nervous. I can also see why it was important for me to dress the part. For the record, I dug out my death suit jacket and paired it with the purple shirt. I hope she noticed, because I'm never wearing this shit again. Not until the next funeral, that is.

"Mr. Green?" her professor says with a smile. "What do you think of Miss Sorensen's design."

"I like it, especially the courtyard, but how much would all that cost?"

Tayler presses on the thing again, and a new slide appears. This one has a breakdown of all the costs associated with her project. She's even gotten it narrowed down by item. There's a price for moving the bar, for getting rid of the narthex thing, for enlarging the kitchen, and for the courtyard. It's astronomical for all of it. But if you start moving shit around inside, you can't just stop on one thing, you'd have to commit to all of it. I listen as Tayler goes through every aspect of the design and why things cost what they do. In all, she's done a really good job. If I did this project, I would know what I was getting into up front.

"Mr. Green?" I look up at Tayler. "What questions do you have for me?"

"If I chose to do the courtyard right now, how would you access it if I didn't do the stuff inside?" Tayler's face falls like I just told her there was no Santa Claus. "I mean, this plan would have to happen in increments. If I started with the outside part of it, how would I do it?"

Her expression changes a little. Not much but some. Tayler uses her clicker to go back to one of the first slides with images of the bar. "You'd have to move the booths here." She points at the screen. "You could cut through the cinderblock and add a doorway there."

"You could check on the permits?"

Tayler gives me a smile. "Of course."

"I think your designs are great, Tayler. If I had more equity in the place, I'd do that in a heartbeat."

"Yes, but think of it this way," she interrupts me. "If you decided to renovate, you'd have more seating and a larger kitchen. More seating alone would enable you to recoup your investment in five years."

She's done her homework. "Can I think about the work inside? I'd like to move forward on the courtyard."

"Great." Tayler's smile is forced. "I'd be happy to work with you on that."

"Well, then...." Her professor stands up and walks to stand next to Tayler. She leans in close to whisper something in Tayler's ear. I can hear her, though. "Next time, don't interrupt the client." Tayler's pretty face falls. "Maybe then he wouldn't have immediately said no."

I need to say something. "I'm not ruling out the entire plan, ma'am. I just need to think about it. This is the first I've seen of her idea, and there's a lot to consider. She obviously knows what she's doing."

I can't tell from Tayler's demeanor if that was helpful or not. I guess I'll have to wait and see.

I wait outside the room for Tayler to appear. When she does, I get a sincere smile. "Thanks, Luke."

I want to wrap her up in a hug, but the bitch professor could come out any minute.

"You did great."

"Yeah?"

"I really did love your ideas. I'm just not sure about the cost. The courtyard was genius."

"I agree. Think about spring through fall. You'd always have people out there on nice days. You could even mount televisions out there for game days."

"Love it." Damn, I want to hug her.

"You look nice, Luke." Her voice is soft, almost hesitant.

"I'm sorry about this morning."

"Me too."

"You were right, though. I would have felt like a dumbass in my T-shirt and jeans."

"I know." Her smile is real. "Sometimes people know more than you."

"People? As in you?"

"In this case, yes. I've been to these presentations before, so I knew what to expect."

"You were nervous."

"That prof hates me."

"Why?"

She shrugs. "No idea."

I whisper in her ear, "She's jealous."

That makes her laugh, which makes me feel better. "She's well respected. And she used to have a show on HomeTV."

"Wow."

"Yeah. She's really good, and I've learned a lot from her. If she thinks my work could be better, then I need to make it better."

We start to walk down the long corridor in the design building when she says, "You really should consider the entire project, though, Luke."

"Can't afford it."

"You can't afford *not* to."

I'm doing my best not to get angry again. "Tayler," I snap. "What I can and can't afford is none of your business."

"Oh, right." She pulls away from me, looking left and then right. "Um, I forgot something back in the room. I'll see you later."

Before I can say another word, she's gone.

CHAPTER TWENTY-SIX

Tayler

I don't know why I'm still putting myself through this with him. Earlier today, when I called myself his girlfriend, he nearly lost his mind. We've been seeing each other exclusively for over a month now. We spend almost every day together. Sometimes it's at work, sometimes it's at my place, and other times it's at his. We've slept in the same bed nearly every night and I'm *not* his girlfriend?

As I sit in my car on the street outside of Cy's, I'm staring at the building I just redesigned. Blinking, I feel my eyes start to burn, but I force back any tears.

But then it hits me. He's right. I'm not his girlfriend. How could I be? We've never *done* anything together. I mean, other than working at the bar, having sex, watching television, and sleeping. He's never taken me out to dinner or to a movie. He doesn't talk about his family, friends, or anyone else for that matter. Hell, I don't even know when his birthday is. And how old is he?

"Shit." A hot tear slides down my cheek.

It's true. I'm *not* his girlfriend. I'm his friend with goddamn benefits.

LUKE: Babe? Quinn's here. You're not coming to work?

I stare at his text message. I was supposed to work at five tonight, but after the epiphany in my car earlier, I decided I couldn't do it, so I started up my car and drove home, stopping first at the store to get ice cream and wine. A necessity for a girl after ending a relationship.

Luke: You okay?

I sigh, knowing I shouldn't have left him in the lurch. In my defense, I called Quinn, who said she'd work for me, thank goodness. She didn't hesitate to say she'd do it—probably because I was sniffling the entire conversation. All she said was "Of course. Should I kill Luke while I'm there?"

That made me laugh. "No." Yes.

I pick up my phone to reply to his text.

Me: We need to talk.

Ha! Now let's see how *he* feels about those four little words.

Luke: Babe. Is this about the bar? Because I don't want to renovate?

God, he's such an asshole. I might as well get it out there. Let him stew for a while.

Me: I can't do this anymore.

Luke: Do what?

Me: Be your fuck buddy.

Luke: Tayler. Is this about the girlfriend bullshit?

I stare at my phone. *Girlfriend bullshit?* No. He. Didn't.

Me: I told you I wasn't going to be your friend with benefits, and that's exactly what I am.

Luke: No. That's not true.

Me: You've never taken me out. I still know nothing about you. Hell, I don't even know your birthday.

Luke: December 11th.

Me: Tomorrow? Your birthday is tomorrow, and you didn't bother to tell me?!

If he could hear my mind, he'd hear screeching. And then he'd hear me cry. How could he not tell me it was his birthday tomorrow?

Oh, I know why he didn't bring it up. It's because I'm just a booty call to him. I mean nothing. And I'm so in love with the jerk, the realization about all of this makes my heart hurt.

Luke: No biggie.

Me: Fuck you. Happy birthday tomorrow, then fuck off after that.

Luke: Babe.

Me: And don't come over after work. Or tomorrow. Or the next day. I'm done. Oh, and I quit.

Luke: What about the courtyard?

Me: You only said you'd do it to be nice.

Luke: No. I want it.

Me: I'll hand over the plans. Hire someone.

Luke: Tayler, come on. Don't be a bitch. I'm too busy to deal with this shit right now.

Don't be a bitch? Christ, I want to punch him in the throat so bad.

Me: Then get to work, asshole. You started this.

And I'm finishing it.

CHAPTER TWENTY-SEVEN

Luke

I know she told me she didn't want to see me, but the second she sent the last text, my head started pounding. I really need to go to my doctor about these headaches. Or maybe a shrink since the only cure seems to be Tayler. Hell, maybe she's the cause too.

Stepping up to Tayler's building, I'm about to call her to let me in, but the door's ajar. It immediately pisses me off. I need to have a word with Vic, her landlord, about this. The door has remained locked pretty much since he installed it after the Dylan episode, but there have been a handful of times that someone has left it ajar, and one time, someone shoved a shoe into the door to keep it from locking.

"I'll deal with that later."

Pulling open the front door, I step through and jog up the steps. It's late, well after two, so I know she'll be asleep. I hope she hears my knock. Raising my hand to the door, I'm about to do just that when I hear voices. Leaning forward, I recognize Tayler right away. The other voice is male. I know that one too. Shit.

Knocking loud and fast, I yell Tayler's name. "Tayler. Open up. It's Luke."

Reaching back, I pull my phone out of my pocket and search for Gage's number. "Be on duty, man."

I quickly knock again. "Open the damn door, Tayler."

Holding the phone up to my ear, I start swearing under my breath before he finally answers. "Gage. It's Luke Green. I think Dylan's at Tayler's place. I've knocked twice. She won't let me in."

"On my way. Knock down the door if you have to."

Knock down the door? My pleasure.

I knock one last time. "Open the goddamn door, or I'm kicking it the fuck down."

I hear the knob jiggle and hold my breath. When it pops open, Tayler's there wearing her normal sleep outfit of shorts and a tee.

I reach out and place my hands on her upper arms. "You okay?"

She nods but then glances to her left. I look over and there that motherfucker is, standing by the windows, hands in his pockets, with a stupid grin on his face. I want to tell him I called the cops, but then he may try to get away. Reaching back, I shut the door, not planning to move any farther into the room until Gage gets here. I don't want to startle the asshole.

"What're you doing here, Dylan?" I growl.

"I just stopped by."

"You're not supposed to 'just stop by,' Dylan. She's got a protective order—"

"I know!" he shouts loudly. "It's bullshit," he snaps.

"It's not bullshit." I look over at Tayler, and I know from her demeanor that she's shaken. "You're scaring her."

"No!" he shouts again. "*You're* scaring her."

I want to laugh at this asshole, but now's not the time for levity. "Why are you here? You know she's with me now."

"You've turned her against me." The snarl in his voice is creeping me out. This dude is definitely unstable.

"No, you did that when you cheated on her." And stalked her.

"It. Was. A. Mistake," Dylan seethes. "How many times do I have to apologize?"

"Dylan." Tayler's voice is soft. "Please...."

Dylan starts to step toward her, snapping, "Please what?"

"Calm down."

"Calm down?" He's still moving our way. "You want me to calm down?"

She nods slowly.

"I'll calm down as soon as *he* leaves." He's pointing at me.

"That's not gonna happen." I look over at Tayler. "How could you let him in?"

The shocked expression on Tayler's face tells me more than I need to know. So when she says, "I thought it was you," I know I shouldn't have said what I said. This isn't her fault.

At that moment, Dylan lunges forward, reaching for Tayler.

Thinking quickly, I pull Tayler back until she's behind me. With me between them, I glare down at him. I've got eight inches on this guy, so I use that to my advantage. My voice is unfamiliar to even me when I grit my teeth and say, "You touch her, I kill you. You got me?"

Holding up both of his hands, he smiles. "Whoa, dude. I just want to talk to my girl."

Did he not hear me?

"*My* girl." I step into his personal space. "How'd you get in the building?"

He shrugs like I just asked him about the weather. "It was unlocked." Dylan tries to step around me, but I move with him.

Tayler's voice is soft. "You need to leave, Dylan."

Dylan's demeanor disintegrates in seconds. "Fucking bitch," he spits as he scrambles to get past me and nearly makes it. He's gotten close enough to take a swipe at her arm, drawing blood.

I grab him by the collar and yank him back. "You fucker." I kick his feet out from under him and slam him down to the floor. I'm on top of him right after that.

"Get. Off. Me," he screams. "I can't breathe."

"Don't care." He's wiggling around like a serpent, but I've got thirty pounds on the guy, so he's not going anywhere.

I look up at Tayler as she asks, "Should I call 9-1-1?"

"Already did. Gage is on his way." And like it was choreographed, we hear urgent knocks on the door. "That's him."

Tayler rushes to the front door, opening it fast. "Gage. Thank goodness."

"You're going to need to press charges this time," Gage says, looking down at Tayler's arm that's now wrapped in white gauze. I helped her wash up and put antibiotic ointment on the wound. "You'll want a doctor to look at that for the report."

I nod. "We'll get that done first thing tomorrow morning."

"I'll go to student health," Tayler says.

"No, we'll go to my doctor."

"I can't afford—"

"I got it. No worries."

She shakes her head but says nothing more about it.

"Have there been any more letters? Other photos?" Gage asks.

"Photos?" *What the hell?*

Tayler shakes her head. "Nothing since the last one."

"Tayler, what are you talking about? What photo?"

She reaches for her phone, and I watch her work the screen. When she's found what she's looking for, she hands me the phone. Using my fingers, I enlarge the image so I can see it's us, Tayler and me. In her bedroom. The night I forgot to wear a condom.

I look up at her, then at the windows, then back at the photo. "This was taken outside your bedroom window."

Gage and Tayler nod.

I stand and quickly walk into her bedroom, heading directly

to the row of windows. It's still dark outside, but I know from the other times I've been here that there are no other three-story buildings nearby, only residential houses. "How?"

"He's got a drone."

I jerk my head to face her. "He has a drone?" I can't believe this shit. "He took photos of us with a drone?"

"Apparently." Gage adds, "Tayler says he received one for Christmas last year."

"He's been surveilling you and this is the first I'm hearing about it?"

Tayler doesn't respond. It's Gage who says, "We decided to deal with this on our own."

God, I'm mad. I don't remember ever being this angry before in my life. "You 'decided to deal with this on your own'?" I scoff. "How'd that work out? Oh, I know. He showed up here like he owns the place, scaring the shit out of Tayler. He's stalking her. You know how dangerous that is? Stalkers like that asshole"—I point out toward the living room, even though Dylan has already been taken into custody by a second officer. "—don't give up. He's unstable. He could have hurt her worse than he did." I can feel the vein in my neck pulsing. "He could have *really* hurt her." And the thought of that nearly undoes me.

I walk over to her and wrap her up in my arms. "I can't stand the thought of someone hurting you, angel."

"It's okay."

It's okay? What the hell kind of response is that? *Ignore it, Luke. Just ignore it. She's been through enough tonight. Hell, today.*

But I can't ignore it.

"It's not okay." And I can't stand the thought of her here alone. Not anymore. "Pack a bag, babe. A big one. You're staying with me."

"No. I'm—"

"That's a good idea, Tayler," Gage cuts in. "A good lawyer

could have Dylan out by tomorrow. You'll be safer at Luke's place. At least until we're sure he's no longer a risk to you."

She sucks in a lungful of air and releases it slowly. "Fine."

Wow. Her excitement is tangible.

Not.

CHAPTER TWENTY-EIGHT

Tayler

"I can't believe I agreed to this." Sure, I'm talking to myself, but I'm okay with that. Luke's left me alone in his bedroom so I can unpack my bag. He's cleared out two drawers for me and half his closet. I don't need anywhere near that kind of space, but it was nice of him. Part of me thinks I should take over his guest bedroom, but I know that won't fly. We still need to talk, though.

I'm exhausted. I look over at his bedside clock and see it's almost sunrise. It's also Luke's birthday.

Stopping my unpacking, I walk down the hallway into the living room. I expected to see him sitting on his sofa, but he's not there. I peek into the kitchen, but he's not there either. When I hear noise coming from the basement, I follow it. I haven't been down here before, so I half expect it to be a moist haven for spiders. Fortunately, that's not the case. He's got a finished family room and what looks like a bedroom and a bath down here as well. Behind another door is a large laundry room.

"Lucky duck."

I hear water running and decide he must be in the shower. I take this as an opportunity. Knocking on the door, I hear him say, "Enter."

Pushing open the door, I marvel at the spa-like bathroom. It's all done in gray and black tones, making it a more masculine design. "This is nice."

"It is. I wish I could tell you I did this, but the basement was done when I moved in."

"Why haven't we hung out down here?"

"I don't spend my time in the basement except to do laundry. I figured you'd want to shower and change up there, so I wanted to give you some space."

"Oh. That was nice." I should have showered, but I did that earlier.

I can see through the clear glass walls. Seeing this man wet, with soapy suds running down his muscular backside, is making me weak in the knees. I should probably go. Getting turned on is not what I or we need right now.

"I'm going to stay here tonight, but after that, I'm going to Cooke and Quinn's."

"No."

I'm shocked by his response. But not so shocked that I can't spit back, "Yes."

"No."

"Luke. Yes. Things with you and me—"

"Are confusing. Besides, I was wrong. You were right."

"Wrong about what?" I shake my head but see, from the corner of my eye, that he's washing his front, all the way down. It's fascinating how thoroughly he's cleaning *everything*. "No. I can't keep doing this with you, Luke. I'm exhausted from it. I'll be better off on my own so I can focus on my work."

I hear the water shut off and watch as he pushes open the door and steps out. Holy shit. I need to avert my eyes because it's like looking into the sun.

Wrapping a towel around his waist, he moves closer. I've got my eyes down, staring at my toes. I need to polish them; they look horrible.

A long finger comes up underneath my chin, pushing my face up until we're eye to eye. "Here's what I propose."

I remain silent.

"I propose you sleep in my room and I sleep on the couch."

"No. Why?"

"I want you to stay with me so I know you're safe. You can cut your hours at the bar if you want so you can focus on school, though you don't have to. If you do that, I'll make you a promise."

"What promise?"

"I promise we'll talk. I mean really talk. I'll take you out. On dates. I'll court you."

I want to scoff, but he looks sincere. "Why now?"

"For one, I was paying attention to your texts tonight. I came over after work to talk to you, to tell you that I wanted to do everything I could to make this right with us. Then, when I heard Dylan's voice through your door, I imagined the worst. That's when it hit me, Tayler. I don't want to lose you. I want you in my life. I've been resisting for a long time, and that's all thanks to my ex-wife."

His *what?* "Your w-wife?" I choke out.

"*Ex*-wife."

"You were married?"

"Yeah. And it fucked me up."

"Ah, I see." I nod slowly. "That makes sense. Dylan's messing with my head too."

"Can we try? Again?"

Holy crap, he looks defeated. "Can we sleep in the same bed? But I agree maybe we should hold off on the sex for a little while. It muddles my thinking."

"Mine too." He smiles. "I'm not sure I can sleep with you without wanting you, but I'll try."

"I want you too." I stare into his pretty eyes. "Do you mean it this time?"

"I do."

"Am I your girlfriend?" Oh, shit. Why do I say stuff like that?

"You're absolutely my girlfriend. You always were. I just have a hard time with labels."

"That means you're my boyfriend."

"I hope so."

Me too.

I lean closer to kiss his lips and say what I came down here to say. "Happy birthday, babe."

"Ah, you remembered."

I roll my eyes and keep the hand I'd like to smack him with at my side. "Funny. Ha ha. If I'd known, I would have gotten you something."

"Birthday's aren't my thing, babe."

"Well, they're mine. I'll make you a cake tomorrow, so tell me your favorite flavor."

"White cake, white icing."

"Really?" That's kind of boring.

"Really."

"As you wish."

He grins. "Maybe celebrating my birthday with you will change my mind."

"Oh, I'll change your mind. Just you wait and see." I smirk.

"I've no doubt. You've already succeeded where all others have failed."

"Why is that, do you think?"

He moves a loose piece of my hair off my face. "Don't know. Something about you that completes me. I'm lost without you. I literally feel ill when you're not around."

"Luke. That's terrible." And sweet at the same time.

"It is what it is. Time for me to stop second-guessing what this is and embrace it."

"So"—I run my hand across his scruffy beard—"do you want me to sing you the 'Happy Birthday' song?"

"Tomorrow. With cake."

"You got it."

Luke leans in and kisses me softly. "Come on. Let's get some sleep."

"Yes, please."

CHAPTER TWENTY-NINE

Tayler: New Year's Even

"Ten, nine, eight, seven, six, five, four, three, two, one... Happy New Year!"

My friends are all celebrating the New Year at Cooke and Quinn's place. Well, Quinn still technically lives with me, but she spends almost every night at this fancy condo. I don't blame her. This place is swanky.

As for me, I'm back and forth between Luke's place and my apartment. We take turns meaning I haven't spent a night alone since the last scare with Dylan. Luke won't let me out of his sight, especially since the semester ended. I've been working most days at the bar; part of that time is helping with the plans for the courtyard. We can't do any construction until spring, but the permits are in order, and I've lined up a crew to do the work. I've even figured out ways to save him a little money. What I haven't been able to do is talk him into any of the other work. He's done a good job not snapping at me about it. And even though I know for a fact that the new plan would generate more money for him, he said he'd rather finish up his house "sometime this century."

I get it.

I need to be happy with the courtyard design. It'll be a feather in my cap when I'm looking for jobs after I graduate in the Spring, so I need to embrace that.

I'm shaken from my thoughts by Quinn. "Happy New Year, love."

She's taken to using Cooke's terms of endearments on me. I don't mind. "Same to you."

"Sad that Luke couldn't make it?"

"Nah, I knew he had to work." I should be there too, but he told me to have fun with my friends and then come to the bar afterward so he can keep an eye on me. "I think I'll take off in a bit, though. They'll probably need help cleaning up." And the faster Cy's gets cleaned up, the quicker we can get home to celebrate New Year's Eve together. "Great party, though, Q. Good work."

"Thanks," Quinn says, beaming.

I reach out and squeeze her hand. "I'm happy for you."

"Same to you. As long as Luke doesn't fuck it up."

"Right?" I smile.

"I'm sorry to ask you this right now, but we haven't talked in forever. Have you seen Dylan lately?"

"No. I know he's still in Ames, but he's staying away from me. I think spending three nights in jail was a wake-up call. I also heard he's seeing someone new." And there's the fact that he's awaiting the hearing. I did press charges. His parents weren't happy about it, so much so that they're no longer speaking to my parents, which is sad, but my folks are on my side. My dad threatened to kick Dylan's ass, but I assured him that Luke was all over it.

Luke finally agreed to meet them, so they drove down and took us out to dinner. I think they liked him, Mom especially. Dad's still wary. I get it. This stuff with Dylan really threw him for a loop.

"Really? Who is he seeing?"

"I'm not sure. I've asked around, but nobody knows."

"I hope it sticks and he leaves you alone."

"Me too."

I suppose you want to know if Luke kept his word about finally opening up to me. The answer is yes, mostly. I still sense he's holding back, but he's trying, which I appreciate. I met his mom and sister at Christmas. His parents are divorced—his mom lives here in Iowa and his dad in California, so he doesn't see much of him. Anyway, I liked his family, and they seemed to like me. I only heard the name Shanna mentioned once or twice. I hope it's because I'm nothing like her. I've seen pictures of her, though. Wedding pictures. To say the two of them were gorgeous together was an understatement. Swear to you, they could have modeled bridal fashions, they were that stunning.

"You okay to drive?" Quinn asks.

Shit. My mind is all over the place tonight. "I'll catch a ride with the others. I hear one of the rugby freshmen is picking us up. He can drop me at Cy's."

"Okay. Text me when you're home safe."

"I will."

"Love you, Quinn."

"Love you back."

I turn to Bull and Robbi. "You guys ready to take off?" I lean in closer and whisper, "I think Cooke wants time alone with his girlfriend." Actually, I know he does. He told me to help him get everyone out. Maybe tonight's the night for my bestie.

It only takes a matter of minutes to get people ready to go. The fact that Quinn was handing out leftovers only sped up the process. Rugby guys are hungry guys.

"Happy New Year, everyone!"

I'm not sure who said it, but we all say it back. I hope they're right. I sure could use a happy New Year.

CHAPTER THIRTY

Luke: New Year's Eve

The ball fell and I watched everyone cheer and kiss, and part of me felt sad as hell. Then I remembered my girl would be here soon and I'd get my New Year's kiss. Even though it's going to be late, I'd much rather kiss Tayler late than never. The thought of never kissing Tayler again makes my head hurt. I know the times I've been away from her; I've felt it physically. So, I'm not doing that anymore. I've learned my lesson. That lesson and the one where I'll do just about anything to make sure she's happy and safe.

Am I ready to talk love yet? No. Even though I'm fairly certain I love her, it's a scary notion. Once you say that four-letter word, shit changes. So no, I'm not ready for that. Am I ready to marry again? I may never be ready to do that, but I am ready to do just about everything else.

"Happy New Year, babe." I feel her hands wrap around me from behind. I place mine on top of hers and smile.

Rotating in her arms, I take her pretty face in my hands and bend down for my kiss. "Happy New Year, angel."

"I missed you," she says softly. It's still crazy loud in the bar, but I could still hear her.

"I missed you more."

"Get a goddamn room!" I turn to see a drunk idiot winding his way toward the narthex. Yeah, I know what that is now.

Tayler and I pull away from each other. "You'd better not be driving!" I shout back.

"No, I'm w-walking, man." He cackles. Then, just before he's out the door, he turns, raises both arms into the air, and screams, "Happy New Year, fuckers!"

The crowd repeats the sentiment, and my girl and I laugh. Then she says the unthinkable. "I adore you, Luke."

Shit. What do I say to that?

"You do?" Nobody has ever said they adored me. I've always been too much of an asshole to be adored. I rather like it. "I can't breathe without you."

I watch Tayler's face change. Her eyes turn glassy, and I swear she's about to cry. "Did I say the wrong thing?" I murmur.

"No." She shakes her head. "You said the perfect thing." She wraps her arms around my waist and pulls me in for a hug, her head resting on my chest. "Thank you, Luke."

Damn. I love this girl. No doubt about it. I mean, how can I not? But I'm not going to tell her tonight. I'll wait until it's just the two of us. I'll make sure it's special.

As special as she is.

EPILOGUE

Tayler: Seven Months Later

When I hear a knock on my front door, I'm surprised. I wasn't expecting anyone, and I know for certain Luke wasn't. Hell, he's still asleep in my bed after having worked until close at the bar. Part of me is a little worried it's Dylan, but he's pretty much left me alone since he was granted probation for the incident in my apartment in December. I also know it's not Quinn because a) she's got a key and b) she's in England with Cooke for another two weeks while he recuperates after getting the brace off. After that, they'll be here for the foreseeable future while he rehabs, which thrills me beyond belief. Life just isn't the same without my best friend.

When the knock sounds again, I'm about to jump up from the couch when Luke, sounding tired, asks, "You want me to get it?"

He knows how I feel about unannounced guests. "No, I'll get it." Standing up from the couch, I walk to the door and peek through the hole. "Oh, it's Gage." That's weird. He doesn't usually just show up. Maybe he's here to see Quinn. Maybe he doesn't know she's in the U.K.

Opening it up, I step aside. "Hi, Gage. What's up?" It's then I see he's in full uniform, which isn't uncommon, but he's not alone. There's another cop right next to him.

Just then, Luke steps up behind me. "Hey, man."

"Uh, hey." Gage sounds, well, nervous.

"Tayler Sorenson?"

Why's he saying my entire name? Weird. "Yes."

"I need to ask you to come with us."

I laugh, thinking it's a joke. "Why?"

The other cop steps up and nudges Gage aside. "Tayler Sorenson, we'd like you to come with us. If you come with us willingly, we won't cuff you."

"Cuff her? What the fuck, Gage?" Luke snaps. "What's going on?"

Gage ignores Luke. "Tayler, where were you last night between the hours of ten and midnight?"

Ten and midnight? "Here."

"Were you here as well, Mr. Green?"

"No. I was at work."

Gage shakes his head. "You were alone, Ms. Sorenson?"

"Yes." I can't believe they're asking me this stuff. "I was alone until Luke got home." I look at the cop I don't know, then back at Gage. "What's going on?"

"Tayler Sorenson," the unfamiliar officer starts, "you're under arrest for the murder of Kara Becker."

I say, "Murder?" at the same time Luke says, "Under arrest?"

This *cannot* be happening.

"Tayler." Luke turns me by my shoulders, forcing me to look at him. I'm in a daze, so it's not easy. "I'll call my lawyer. Just go with them. But, babe?" He sounds foreboding. "Say. Nothing."

"But I didn't do anything."

"I know, but promise me you'll wait for the attorney."

I nod and step out into the hallway.

"I'll be right behind you. Don't worry, Tayler."

Easy for him to say. He's not under arrest for murder.

Coming soon... *Deadhead: Bedhead Book 3*

ACKNOWLEDGMENTS

Thank you to Kristen and Kim, for editing this book from start to finish.

And an extra special thank you to Becky Johnson at Hot Tree Promotions for your advice, expertise, and her positivity.

And for my beta readers, Kay and Elizabeth. Thank you so much for your time and feedback!

BOOKS BY KAYT MILLER

The Palmer Sisters

Lainie

Agatha

Sadie

Cortland

Keely

Violet

Molly

Standalones

The Art of the Game

The Virginia Chronicles

One of a Kind

The Portrait Painter

Game Changer

Bedhead

FarmBoy

The Flynns

Out of the Blue

Mick'sology

Vested Interest

The Importance of Being Ernie with Bonus Book The Importance of Being Kennedy's

Quirky Girl

For a complete list of Kayt's books, visit:

Kayt's Website: kaytmiller.com

ABOUT THE AUTHOR

Kayt grew up in the midwest surrounded by a loving family which included three brothers, one sister, and parents who always fostered her creative side.

Kayt wrote her first book when she couldn't find a story about a certain type of a woman and a specific kind of man. She called it *Game Changer* and it couldn't have been a more appropriate title. It changed her life in many ways.

Her goal, as a writer, is to write stories that relate to all of us, to make readers laugh and maybe cry sometimes. Kayt hopes her readers can escape into a fantasy, one that's actually possible. Sure, some of the stories are dubbed "Insta-love" but that's okay. She fell in love with her husband pretty damn fast and with her daughter the second she saw her.

Please Follow Me on these social media sites. Following on BookBub to learn about special book deals.

I love hearing from you!

 facebook.com/authorkaytmiller

twitter.com/kaytmiller1

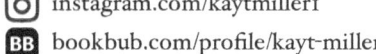 instagram.com/kaytmiller1

bookbub.com/profile/kayt-miller

THANK YOU!

Thank you so much for reading Tayler and Luke's story!

When I start a story, it begins with an outline, notes, and lots of crazy thoughts running through my head. When I actually start writing, the characters take over, leading me through the story like they're holding my hand—guiding me. The process is exciting and cathartic. With that said, I hope you enjoy the story.

If you did, please go to my website, www.kaytmiller.com, and join my newsletter so you can be the first to know what's coming up next. And...

Please, leave a review!

COMING SOON: DEADHEAD

Bedhead Book Three

Stay tuned for Book Three in the Bedhead Series...

**Gage Golden finally gets the girl.
The question is which one?
And at what cost?**